LET THE

GAME

COMMENCE

THE NEW THRILLER FROM
DAVID PALIN

Published in 2022 by
Matthew James Publishing Ltd
Unit 46 Goyt Mill
Upper Hibbert Lane
Marple
SK6 7HX

www.matthewjamespublishing.com

ISBN: 978-1-913230-56-2

Typeset in the UK

CHAPTER 1

Merryking Close – to the local estate agents, the opportunity of a sale in that exclusive, pedestrianised street means all their Christmases have come at once; a very Merryking Christmas. Not that there is anything particularly spectacular about the properties, but as can happen, a part of town known for its fading, frayed grandeur has become fashionable again, moneyed; a place of upward mobility rather than nobility, often to the annoyance of those who have lived there happily for years and have no desire for their council tax and other costs to go up. Every old city has those revitalised suburbs. Perhaps only in Edinburgh might the buyer think twice about moving to this particular address, the sound of the name evoking a dark past. But here, the full gamut of estate agency clichés can be applied, verging, as so often, on the fraudulent, or geographically imaginative as and when a property becomes available, though that is rare, given there are only seven houses.

There are unwritten rules to be kept to in the Close; colours not to be used. It seems nothing other than white on the mock-classical main structures will do. The iron railings and front doors glint with a deeper blackness than the heart of a futures investor. Standards must be met, on the outside at least.

One house appears to have let things slip, judging by the rust on the railings, the flaking paintwork on walls and door. If the residents of the Close actually spoke to each other, someone might have complained, but there seems little interaction between the neighbours – on the surface at least.

Not much is known about the rather reclusive owner of Number Three.

That will change.

Potential is the word the estate agents would use to market that property, accentuating the positive. Quite what terminology the sales rep would use to describe the spatters of blood on one of the bedroom windows, is unknown.

*

Some time before

It was safe.

From her position parked fifty yards down the adjoining road, she had watched that miserable old bitch who lived across the way from her stagger onto a bus and head off into town.

It was ironic – for a street where the residents rarely interacted, it was difficult to avoid people's attention, in particular from behind their twitching curtains. But for now, they were all out, or if the warehouseman was home, he would be asleep after his night shift. Her husband was off doing...whatever he did. They talked little these days. It seemed he worked just to fund his dream, which he never deigned to share with her. Whatever it was, she doubted it would ever become a reality, at least not in her lifetime, so she had grown tired of there never being enough money; of him locking himself away in the attic with his hopes and his toys, while her cellar remained unvisited. This very moment wouldn't be happening if it weren't for his lack of attention.

Is that right, Helen – is that really true?

The hand moving now along her thigh and her body's response to it provided her with all the answer she needed.

"Is it safe now?" His words, more or less echoing her thoughts, were tinged with impatience, while the tracing of his finger heightened hers.

"Yes, let's go – but just in case, let's stick to the plan."

Despite his frustrated shrug, he remained in the car while she made her way to the house and let herself in. A few minutes later the doorbell rang. In a moment of remote distraction, she noted that his mouth was on hers even before the door swung shut. He took her hand, started leading her towards the stairs, but she was nervous, perhaps paranoid, and went through to the lounge. He followed her and to her embarrassment, she could see the surprise on his face as he took in the surroundings.

"You said he earns how much?"

She watched him touch the worn chair covers, his distaste apparent, and saw the thinly veiled disdain as he noticed the dated décor and light fittings. Her discomfort gave rise to a misplaced, nonsensical defensiveness. "He's a highly qualified engineer. The thing is, he has this project – he's quite secretive about it and disappears up into the loft for hours and..."

His lips cut her short and her sudden hunger now matched his. She led the way back out and up the stairs. He undressed her by the bed and she him. God, what an undiscovered country he had brought her to, or at least one that had become overgrown since last visited. When had she last felt... that there... and that?!

With his lips composing a symphony on her body, it was some time before she opened her eyes.

She'd not heard a thing. Was this her conscience? No, that shotgun looked real enough.

She gasped, screamed, started to struggle her way back up the bed. Assuming these were responses to his tongue, her lover strengthened his grip on her hips as she pushed his face away.

"Please!...I'm sorry...I'm so sorry!...Please!"

"So am I," came the whispered response, the emotion in those three words suggesting they were heartfelt and full of grief.

The barrels, which had been pointing towards the floor, lifted slowly – a barrier allowing Death to pass through.

*

The day started as it would end: with a bang.

His eyelids flew open like an old, plastic baby doll's. Arthur Du Fuss's immediate visceral reaction was excitement, but then reality began to throb like an ancient, deep scar, which he had aggravated by waking. Arthur breathed deeply. He looked to the right, forgetting, as always, that he had slept for years in a single bed, reached for and, thanks to his shaking hands, knocked to the floor a photo frame which had been standing on the bedside table. Dismayed, he picked it up; studying it for a moment he laid tender fingertips on the picture, saying: "Good morning, my darling Helen."

For once, there was not the usual smothering sense of panic to which he had awoken every morning since she had left him, so he grew calmer. He had new plans, but first there were old rituals to observe while he garnered the necessary reserves of courage.

Now he stared left towards the window. Hearing heels on the pavement and, with that, knowing the source of the loud noise which had woken him, he thrust off the blankets and pushed aside the fraying curtains just in time to see her feet disappearing behind a forsythia bush.

*

Yvonne Elmer slammed her front door, phone, as usual, already pincered between her perfect brunette bob and the shoulder of her smart, dark-blue power suit – a last glance in the hallway mirror on leaving had assured her, as ever, of those adjectives vital to her appearance – before striding with purposeful confidence down the Close.

"We can discuss this when I get in, Charles. We'll advise them to sue; this violates antitrust laws big time. You know me Charles – as..." She broke off as she passed Number One and allowed the phone to drop away from her ear. Her pace slowed, despite her best efforts. "Fuck!" It was a whisper.

At the window of the end house stood Sandra O'Reilly, gazing out in all her forty-something blonde brassiness. Her blouse was open, revealing an impressive cleavage, which she boosted further by folding her arms beneath her bra, before giving a taunting smile, accompanied by an exaggerated blown kiss.

Yvonne lowered her gaze. A tinny voice reminded her she was mid-call and, doing her best to regain her composure, she picked up her pace and her conversation. "Um, anyway Charles, I'll be in ASAP. Ciao."

With that, she tossed her attaché case onto the passenger seat of a sporty midnight-blue BMW in a reserved parking space, sank into the soft cream leather and drove off after a last glance back in the direction of Number One.

*

"Ah, Miss Elmer. I nearly missed you."

Arthur observed the little episode unfold in front of Number One and gave a knowing smile. He caught a fleeting glance of the blue BMW through the opening in the boundary wall as Yvonne drove off and then leant towards the window. "Goodbye, Miss Elmer."

Today in particular, he wanted to see them all. Count them all out before he drew them all in. He was grateful that she had slammed her front door with her usual brio. Arthur had never needed an early morning alarm call for as long as Yvonne Elmer had been charging her legal fees in the city, her job requiring her to leave at this appropriately ungodly hour.

Arthur, or Art as he would have been known by friends if he had any, knew that now he had time to make a cup of tea before the next departure. He turned from the window, smirking, but that expression faded as he looked once more at the photo by his bed.

Somewhere in the house a clock chimed. Arthur stared towards the sound, swallowing hard. He picked up his watch from a dresser and took a somewhat unnecessary look at the time as he strapped it on. Pulling on a dressing gown, he shuffled downstairs.

Having filled the kettle, Arthur picked out a mug that bore the legend 'Abandon Ye hope, all who are interred here'. Despite everything, he had to smile. Helen had bought the mug – too many years ago – when the local undertakers had made an admirable, but ultimately futile attempt to sex up their business. How she had laughed. Perhaps their efforts were misguided, but when you worked day in, day out in that environment, you must have needed the comic relief. Arthur believed that the burden on the bereaved was onerous enough, so what was wrong with a touch of black humour to match the armbands? There was always someone who complained or resisted in these politically correct times. Now he remembered receiving an internal email in error from a blind charity to which he had subscribed, discussing an upcoming forest walk and the need to approach the families for donations. The writer had outlined how his colleagues would recognise the relatives because 'they would be the ones not bumping into the trees'. Arthur hadn't made any fuss, just responding to the sender with a cautionary but light-hearted comment about taking better care with predictive addresses. Others might have been dusting off their soapbox for that before hitting the bottom half of the internet.

He put the mug down with a crash of sudden anger.

"Cocksuckers! Never heard of graveyard humour?" In its own way it fed an appetite every bit as sharp as that which was satisfied by the post-funeral sandwiches and the small talk. The proof was there in his smile now, for he could smile, even though he felt the ache of her absence, and their abrupt parting, more every day.

He gathered himself together and looked towards the window.

"Well..." He gave a rueful smile. "Just you wait."

The demented whistling of the kettle brought him back to immediate needs. Having poured the water, he put one sugar in his tea and then, with a rueful grin, put in another two for the hell of it. His heart was strong enough. Too damn strong. It had survived being broken – and worse.

He had to move on. Things to do. He carried his mug through into the lounge, drew back the old velvet drapes, and took his usual seat facing the window. On cue, the door to Number Two opened. "Now, will it be both of you this morning?" he said, as he peered through the yellowing lace curtain.

*

13

Emma Thomas wasn't having this now. She tugged her arm out of Darren's none-too-friendly grip, though part of her – the part she sometimes wished held less sway in her blood – couldn't help but admire the way the sleeves of his plaid shirt stretched across his bicep. She stepped out into the morning chill and he followed.

His voice took on a more conciliatory tone. "I'm just saying, it would have been nice if just this once you didn't do the overtime, especially..." He made to step forward, turned and pulled at the lead being stretched in the opposite direction by a rather reluctant Jack Russell – "C'mon Biggles, for fuck's sake!" – before slamming the door shut.

Emma looked around at the other houses. She knew already, judgemental eyes would be taking stock. "Keep your voice down!" she hissed. "And don't take it out on the dog." She gestured towards their house. "Look, it's the overtime that helps us afford this. I've worked hard to get where I am... and we are. Freight forwarding may not be very glamorous, the hours are demanding, but it can be rewarding; it needs commitment and my team needs me."

"So, who's this meeting with?"

"It's just a meeting! What is wrong with you? You're always so bloody jealous."

She turned on her heels and started to storm off, though it was as much about escape as anything. Self-righteousness and guilt were uneasy but common bedfellows – the irony of that particular image didn't escape her – and she knew her eyes might betray her.

"Look," she heard Darren take a deep breath, trying to calm down, "all I'm saying is, we don't often have shifts that coincide. It would have been nice to spend the evening together. That's all."

She stopped, considered for a moment the huge gains to be made and decided to follow in the footsteps of antiquity, which led so often to the downfall of men. Putting on a disingenuous smile, she turned, walked back to her husband and kissed him, adding a little nip on the bottom lip.

"I'll be home in time for cocoa." She kissed him again, the bite a little more protracted this time. "Then it's just you and me."

She saw how his smile spoke of both victory and weakness. Now she stooped, took a playful grab of Biggles's snout and pretended to kiss it. "Bye-bye Biggles – you be a good boy at Nana's. You're a good boy – yes you are."

With that, she headed off again down the Close, turning once to give Darren a little wave before continuing on her way.

She knew the skirt and jacket were moulded to her curves, perhaps a little too much so in recent times, which was something she would address at the gym, and was aware of their impact – not just on her husband. When she passed Number Six, she glanced up with care and gave her brightest smile as she saw him looking out. Now she gave a discreet downward pull of the jacket to further accentuate her bust. Turning to check Darren had gone, she then gave a little wave and hurried on. Her admirer broke off from combing his abundant locks to grant her a wink.

*

As Darren watched Emma go, his smile faded and some shadow crossed his features before he turned and headed in the opposite direction with Biggles towards his car.

*

Indeed, it was both of them this morning. Arthur leaned forward, observing the performance. They worked shifts and today it seemed their schedules coincided. That would probably ruin her plans, he thought, and chuckled. So, it was no surprise to observe the tension and their less-than-fond farewell. From behind them came the dog, towed along with great reluctance. The poor beast never knew whether it was coming or going. It would have to spend today with the in-laws. Once Emma had used the main weapon in her – in every woman's – armoury, namely male weakness, to pour oil on troubled waters, Darren Thomas kissed his thirty-something wife goodbye and headed towards the main street, where his car was parked, while Emma made her head-turning progress in the other direction towards the garages at the end of the Close, where her own Mercedes was housed. Only Arthur saw the tension in her husband's smile and the poorly feigned insouciance of Emma's glance up at the windows of Number Six. Yet he knew that his would not be the only pair of eyes watching her departure.

Sure enough, he saw the curtains in Number Four twitch as the rheumy, jaundiced windows to the envious soul of Celia Braddock followed Emma Thomas' firm, rounded, well-pummelled buttocks on their swaying journey down the Close.

"Better keep the dog safe, Darren." He loved being the keeper of Celia's other secret, regretted that there was no-one here in the Close with whom he could share that.

Now Celia reappeared, closing her front door and lurching towards the road in a long, dark coat that covered a pronounced stoop. He didn't bother to hide from her behind his curtains and she glared at him as she went.

"Go on, go and spit your poison far and wide," he sneered, "while you still can."

The old bitch was off to do her weekly shop, spreading joy amongst checkout staff, shelf stackers and bus passengers everywhere. He had chosen this day of the week for the very reason that the all-seeing harridan would be out and therefore would not be the first to know. If nothing else could destroy the cantankerous witch, the knowledge that she had not been able to break the news of the upcoming event in the Close might just do it. Arthur sipped his tea and grew more resolute. Already, the behaviour of the neighbours on leaving their homes in this select mews for the day, further reassured him that his decision was vindicated.

He must have dozed for a moment, because he jumped when another door slammed, the reverberations echoing through the less than perfect soundproofing of his supposed des res. Arthur had often noticed how the brick walls at either end of the Close seemed to trap all sound, causing it to echo. Yet though the height of that brickwork enhanced a sense of seclusion and exclusivity, this could sometimes turn to a feeling of isolation once the sun had set.

He turned towards the source of the sound.

*

Sandra O'Reilly assessed herself in the mirror, taking in the short skirt, sexy knee-high boots and giving her hair a final tweak, before coming to her usual conclusion and addressing her reflection: "So, who'll be the lucky one this weekend? Did I say 'one'? Must be getting old."

She gave the skirt the slightest downward tug, more in appreciation of her flat stomach than out of any sense of decorum. Now she picked up her coffee mug and cigarette, took a drag on the latter and looked around her lounge, on almost every surface of which stood porcelain collectibles. Wandering around the room, she made minute adjustments to the positioning of a couple of ornaments.

Only when she stopped by a particular cabinet did her features darken. On one shelf there was an obvious gap amongst the group of figures representing the tale of Cinderella. Even Sandra noticed the shaking of her hand as she took another lungful of smoke.

She glanced at her watch, tutted, grabbed her Louis Vuitton overnight bag and headed for the door.

*

Ah, here was someone whose life was probably as lonely as his: Miss O'Reilly. Blimey O'Reilly - Arthur chuckled even though that same epithet came to him every time he saw her. "Should have changed your surname by deed poll to Orally - I bet it's much more appropriate."

He laughed with contempt as she appeared, teetering out on her tart-heels with her ostentatious bag, nearly stumbling as she ditched her cigarette butt and tried to step on it with all the finesse of someone on stilts.

"Off for another weekend on your back?"

As if she heard him, Sandra O'Reilly stopped and glanced in his direction. She bent to adjust her shoe-strap, making a point of allowing a view down her blouse. Then she looked up, straight at him it seemed, and mouthed words that might have been 'fucking old creep' before smoothing her hair. Now she headed towards the spot where he knew she parked her bright red Audi TT.

Despite everything, Arthur was a little shaken by that interaction, but his solace lay in what the day would hold for all of these nouveau riche peasants. All Sandra O'Reilly had to show for being the manageress of a highly successful estate agency was her car and that shrine to the great god of collectibles in which she lived. Arthur had never been invited in - not been anywhere in a long time - but he just knew that the bad taste on display in her home would have overwhelmed him to the point of vomiting. Judging by the number of parcels she received, her collection must have dominated her rooms. Doubtless each item was numbered and tagged, but he knew one was missing and that its absence probably caused that chest of which she was so proud to constrict each day. Stupid bitch, trying to fill the emptiness around her. He wondered whether any of the parcels contained a replica, special edition Victorian dildo for those lonely evenings. He couldn't understand it; she was not an unattractive woman. He paused and took a deep breath to try to stop himself retching.

Turning away from the window, he caught sight of another photograph of Helen on the mantelpiece. Shamefaced, he reflected on how he had just allowed the image of Miss O'Reilly's spread legs, and the faint penile twitch that it had caused, to infect the space that he had shared with his beloved woman. He closed his eyes and a tear rolled down his mottled cheek. When he opened them, he was still looking in the direction of his deceased wife's picture. An image flashed in front of him and he squeezed his eyes shut against the force of it.

"Forgive me," he said, out loud this time in a quivering voice. "Forgive me for everything."

A movement on the edge of his vision rescued him from weakness, yet caused his heart to sink as he turned back to the road.

"Ah, Mr Hansen."

*

Andrew Hansen rushed out of his house, pulling a bomber jacket over his fashionably half-untucked shirt. Now he turned and leaned back through the front door. "C'mon Sally,

I'm running a bit late." He gave a hurry-up gesture, took a peek in the window to ensure everything about his fledgling man-beard and coiffure – could the haircut of any young guy be seen as anything else in these times? – was in place and walked away down the Close while stuffing a sheaf of papers into a folder, only to turn again on hearing his front door being slammed with some force. The girl responsible glared at him.

"It's Sarah!"

"Just testing." He had the grace to look sheepish, but a part of him was also trying to remember which one was Sarah!

He smiled and as ever was surprised to see the impact of that facial gesture. Andrew loved the opposite sex, but his success with them remained a puzzle to him. He knew he could be charming and had received enough compliments in his time to know he wasn't without some appeal, but was the world so full of arrogant Lotharios that an IT geek with some homespun cheek could name his prize?

Even now, Sarah's anger seemed to be dissipating as she scurried after him, tying up her hair, addressing both herself and the world: "Only myself to blame, I suppose."

He put his arm around her; there was some token resistance and then she allowed him to kiss her.

*

Arthur looked on and there was sorrow in his next words: "Another heart broken, young Andrew?"

There he went, rushing down the Close, late as usual. Now Arthur managed to smile, almost indulgent and more than a touch wistful. He knew little about Andrew, a lot less than he had once hoped, except that he when returned home, it was often with his arms full of books or a girl. He seemed to go through both in great numbers. Not such a bad lad though.

Arthur crossed the room and picked up a single dog-eared Christmas card next to the photograph of Helen. He read, before gesturing with it towards the photo, smiling: "He, at least, made an effort once upon a time."

A look of deep pain twisted his features as he remembered: how Andrew had popped greetings cards though all the letter-boxes on the Close that first Christmas after he had moved in; how Arthur had popped round to thank him and welcomed him for a drink any time.

How five years had passed.

He wandered back to his chair, took his weary seat again and sipped at his tea.

As Andrew Hansen walked past the window, Arthur had wondered whether he would look across at all in his direction. How he wished for it, but dreaded it too, for it would have weakened his resolve. But Andrew had continued on his way, fiddling with the flaps of his jacket pockets, staring straight ahead towards the main road and passing up the chance to change so many lives.

Another door closed, slammed by someone on whom no melancholy would be wasted. Arthur's expression soured. He rose again from his seat and tweaked back the net curtain.

*

Brad Llewellyn stepped out, adjusting his cuff-links, talking loudly into a mobile phone wedged between shoulder and chin as he went.

"Look, it's pretty simple, Hugo – either the file is on my desk by the time I get in, or he's fired. Comprendez? ... I don't know – that's what I pay you for ... oh, I'll use tact, don't worry. I'll say 'you're tin tacked'." He smirked at his own joke before continuing. "I mean, I'm not made of money. Okay, I'll be in after I've called at the racecourse. Gotta get the tickets for the event next week. I know... they're such mugs... a day at the races, a free bar and a chicken Caesar salad and they're putty in your hands. Ciao."

Standing now by his Porsche, he straightened his shirt collar until the correct amount showed above his Armani jacket. His gelled hair barely moved in the morning breeze; still, he could not resist looking at his reflection in the car window and tweaking it.

*

Arthur dropped the net curtain in disgust.

"When you next have your mane tended, see if they can't geld you as well."

As if in response, the air was filled by the roar of an engine and the screeching of tyres, doubtless sending a middle finger of smoke and fumes into the face of environmentalists everywhere as the Porsche sped away.

As far as Arthur could tell, there were two types of entrepreneur and you could judge them by the time of their departure from home. As usual, Brad Llewellyn was late leaving

Number Six. Arthur despised him. Nothing wrong with owning your own business, but Llewellyn threw his money and his, or other people's, women around with brutish, swaggering arrogance. Even on this exceptional day, Arthur was unable to measure the depth of his contempt for the greying stallion that had preened and strutted, designer-clad, down the Close in front of him.

Still, if there was one thing worse than the man who ate another man's food, it was the man who didn't notice that his food was being eaten. And from what Arthur could hear sometimes in the revealing acoustics of the Close, there was one pot that was regularly being licked clean.

Far worse than the ostentatious revving that had accompanied the departure of the Porsche was the silence that descended now on Merryking Close. So, that was the last of them. Now the Close was deserted except, as so often, for Mr Arthur Du Fuss. No-one left.

No more excuses.

Arthur glanced again at his watch. He stood, and as he lifted his mug to drain the last of the tea, noticed that his hands were shaking. He had things to do to prepare.

But first a spot of breakfast. A little bit of everything that he enjoyed.

Arthur drew the velvet drapes again across the square of light that had become his world, plunging the room into darkness, and headed for the kitchen.

CHAPTER 2

Sepp Stoehlheim lifted the fine white Dresden china cup to his lips and sipped at the coffee, which as ever was cooling way too quickly in his air-conditioned office. The luxurious red, damask drapes held the morning sunshine at bay, so the only light came from the desk anglepoise and his computer, throwing shadows across his imposing aquiline features. He stared at the polished skull *memento mori* on his luxury walnut desk and then leant back in his chair, turning it so as to take in the picture on his wall, Munch's *The Scream*, which as ever held his attention and caused a thin smile; the closest mankind had ever come to capturing the unimaginable truth.

Stoehlheim made to take another sip of coffee – and slammed down the cup, throwing back his head, neck arching, eyes screwed shut, as the shock flared in his skull, burrowing down his spine. His grimace was a mocking mirror of the death rictus, which he had seen so often. This dark gift was a curse, a joke prolonged by a palsied and increasingly bitter God.

He opened his eyes again and addressed his tormentor: "Are you not tired yet of this... demonstration of your waning powers?"

The aftershock subsided and he could tell by the severity of the spasms that the end was near. Soothed by the comfort of that anodyne thought, he took tissues from a silver case on his desk and started to mop up the spilled coffee. These frustrating, weakening attacks were reason enough for him to keep his office door closed. Examining his shirt-front and cuffs, his silk tie and Hugo Boss jacket, he sighed with relief. "Gott sei dank!" he said under his breath – no coffee stains.

Now his drop-dial clock sounded a Westminster chime. Stoehlheim glanced across: the hands read 8 a.m. precisely. It was coming. Who would it be?

He rose from his seat and crossed to a cabinet, on which stood a model of Justice, blindfolded, sword and scales in hand. Grinning, he picked up the statue, which seemed small in his large hand and addressed it: "To what will you turn a blind eye today?"

*

Arthur's hands shook all through breakfast. He had dropped three matches before he was able to light the grill for the toast. Also, he felt an a deeper than usual seasonal chill, and no matter how much coke he threw into the boiler, it seemed unable to warm his bones, even though he could feel the heat scorch his skin when he opened the hatch. He wondered for a distracted moment whether the flames of Hell burned your flesh and froze your bones at the same time. Now that would be torment indeed.

The piece of toast quivered in his fingers. When it turned to ash in his mouth, he placed it back on the plate. Now he

26

needed both hands to try to steady the mug of coffee with which he sought to wash away the dryness in his throat.

He had to face facts at last – he'd been deluding himself; he couldn't go through with it. As each of his neighbours had departed that morning, leaving the world to darkness and to him, so a layer of resolve had disappeared with them, exposing his great scheme as nothing more than bitter scribblings. He stood. No, he would call...

The grandfather clock in the hall struck nine.

Arthur's head jerked in the direction of the chiming. It couldn't have chilled him more if it had struck midnight and he had turned to find the ferryman standing there, palm outstretched in expectation of a coin. There was no element of chance in that timing. The hour was approaching and the guardians of the world that lies beyond our sight, but not our senses, were reminding him.

Having given up on breakfast, Arthur headed through the prevailing gloom of the sombre house to the bathroom. Little daylight filtered through the velvet drapes. A warm bath worked some magic, providing a degree of atavistic comfort and relaxation, and now he stood at the cracked washbasin. He stared for a moment or two at the mirror, at the face and world that was his and yet not; every detail the same, but false. With a rueful smile he contemplated the absurdity of shaving, yet went ahead and did it anyway, ensuring a smooth, close shave unlike so many men of his age. The clock struck the half-hour, startling him enough that he cut himself. He stopped the bleeding with a piece of tissue and then found himself almost mesmerised by the stain. A glance at his watch showed him there was still time.

Back in his bedroom, Arthur removed his freshly laundered, guards cut pin-striped suit from his wardrobe. This he put on, along with a white shirt, shoes polished to mirror-like perfection and a yellow and grey striped tie, knotted in a perfect Windsor. It didn't matter what you got up to in your attic; when outsiders came into your house, there were standards to keep. After a glance in the mirror, accompanied by a nod of approval, he opened a drawer and removed a key, which he slipped into his pocket.

"Now for the tough bit."

Arthur could not decide whether the words were laced with bitter irony or a simple statement of bare, stone-cold fact...

...and he would never know.

CHAPTER 3

Declan Donaghue entered the offices of 'Stoehlheim and Stoehlheim', for once welcoming the subdued, somewhat funereal lighting as he stepped out of the bright winter sunshine. He wasn't feeling so good; it had been a heavy night. That was one of the dangers of working in the city – after work you headed for the bars, allowing the rush hour to pass. At least that was what the trainee alcoholics told themselves.

As he yawned, he kept a wary eye on the door to the inner office. He knew that his condition and demeanour would not go down very well with old Stoehlheim, that immaculate, groomed stickler for Teutonic formality and old-world etiquette. Declan guessed he could understand that. On the whole, the legal profession got a pretty bad press, but clients were a strange lot, who appeared to accept being screwed if you looked the part. Twenty pounds for drafting a letter on their behalf with civility, in a three-piece charcoal pin-stripe – that they could live with. Of course, in most instances they had little choice, hence the reputation of lawyers had not moved too far forward into the light since the days of Bleak House. The charge for which young Declan had no understanding was for receiving letters; doing so in a red-eyed, curried sweat was therefore a definite no-no. He wasn't looking unkempt by choice, but had overslept. Knowing that arriving late at this establishment was akin to handing in your resignation, much of his getting dressed that morning had been performed in the car, using traffic jams to his benefit.

Edward Booth-Catesby, one of the other young lawyers, looked up and gave a muted "Good morning" – as the youngest qualified lawyer he was the first in, preparing his own path for the day, and also those of some senior colleagues who never hesitated to take advantage. His greeting was then followed by a scything movement of hand across his throat. Declan panicked – was he already in some sort of trouble? But he had misinterpreted; when the gesture was repeated, he realised Edward was signalling that his tie and top shirt-button were still undone. He rectified that in double-quick time, though it was rare for Stoehlheim to wander out amongst his minions. Their mentor's world was the very definition of business behind closed doors; well, a particular door, though 'mahogany edifice' was perhaps a more appropriate description.

Declan picked up the post from the tray by the entrance – distributing it was a task allocated to the most junior member of the team – dumped it on his desk, and flicked on his computer before heading for the coffee machine, where Edward joined him. Though a couple of years older than Declan, they had a good relationship, Edward having been the most recent colleague to complete the pupillage.

There was a proper Tchibo filter and a Krupps espresso maker. Old Stoehlheim considered this to be a country of Philistines where coffee was concerned and he had certainly forked out to ensure that his morning cup was of the same high quality as in the land of his fathers. Declan opened the tin of Guatemalan – there was already a jugful prepared, but he knew more would always be needed, given the hours worked. The aroma lifted his spirits. He set up everything.

Edward had dug out a cup for himself. Now he looked at Declan and grimaced, fished in his pocket and drew out a piece of chewing gum, which he handed across, saying: "Better chew while you can."

Both of them glanced at the yellow strip emanating from the bottom of Stoehlheim's door. Declan leaned forward.

"What do you..." he started to whisper, but Edward made a hushing gesture of finger to lips and responded even more softly.

"Firstly, I don't know how he does it, but he seems to hear everything." He looked around. "Perhaps this place is even bugged. But secondly, your breath stinks of garlic." Now he held his cup towards Declan, though with a smile.

Having poured their respective coffees, Declan returned to his seat. It was still early, half past seven. The desk lamp poured a honeyed glow onto the blotter. It never entered anyone's head to offer Stoehlheim a coffee. No-one risked disturbing him, not even knocking to say "Good morning". Stoehlheim had made it clear that initiating pleasantries, if at all, was his prerogative.

Declan flicked through the post. The envelopes passed before his eyes like a slide show, the address on each of them prompting him to think about the firm of 'Stoehlheim and Stoehlheim'. Who was the other half of that partnership? A son or brother perhaps? There were no photographs in Stoehlheim's office to indicate any familial ties. His boss was an intensely private man, with the emphasis on intense.

Knowing that this particular avenue of thought would lead down a cul-de-sac, Declan turned to contemplating himself, which was every young man's right. Weighed against the early start and the lack of warmth from his employer was, he acknowledged, an excellent all-round legal training at the hands of his experienced and seemingly omniscient mentor. Remuneration was excellent. When he talked with friends who were also doing pupillages, not one was on the same level of commission, expenses package, or basic salary. Research into the company showed it to be long-established to say the least, and financially very sound. Also, 'Stoehlheim and Stoehlheim' had an unparalleled track record, winning cases against all the odds. It was as if the Stoehlheims had the ear of every judge worth knowing.

Belonging to this practice appeared to be an elite position. Pupillages were not always available here, but Declan had discovered that when they were, they carried with them the opportunity to join the firm upon completion of one's studies. It was strange then how few people appeared to have actually taken up these offers, perhaps because Stoehlheim was such a cold fish, or more likely because the firm was very demanding. Declan remembered being summoned to the office at six-thirty in the morning and then summarily despatched to a police station one hundred miles away to interview a client whom he discovered later was in reality a small-time, would-be gangster. The station had no officers to spare, so Declan had sat alone with him. The man had been prone to sudden, aggressive outbursts, leaping up more than once to pace around the small interview room, swearing vengeance on those who had shopped him and on humanity in general. The experience had been one of huge discomfort and stress. Only the smooth silkiness of the Audi's suspension on the drive home and the glint of his Tag Heuer watch had calmed Declan, reminding him of the potential rewards ahead, material at least.

He had never warmed to any of the other lawyers in the firm, but admired and aspired to their drive and expertise, as well as their sartorial elegance, which appeared, almost without exception, to mirror that of Stoehlheim himself. If Declan envied anything about the man, it was his wardrobe.

The coffee machine spat as the last of the water drained through the filter. Declan was feeling weary. The cup he had been sipping while flicking through the post was empty, so he pushed back his chair and was about return to the machine when a particular, rather unusual letter caught his eye.

For a start, the envelope was handwritten, and that hand had been shaking. Slitting it open, he started to read the contents. His chewing stopped, in part because his mouth had fallen open as he read, then re-read, the scrawled handwriting. Throwing himself back down in his seat, he leant forward and rested his forehead on his fingertips, taking in everything one more time. There was no mistake. It said what it said. Now there was a dilemma. This had to be taken straight to the top.

Except...

He glanced at his Tag Heuer and whispered: "Still time!" Now he stared with indecision yet again at the strip of light from Stoehlheim's door.

He stood and straightened his tie. Spitting out the chewing gum, he concealed it in a scrap of paper before binning it. With great hesitation he headed for that inner office, stuffing the letter into his jacket pocket.

Fighting the chill of irresolution, he lifted his hand as if contemplating knocking on that door. However, his movement was stayed by a horrified whisper from across the office as Edward hissed: "What the hell are you doing? Have you gone mad!?"

If anything summarised both the surreal mist in which that company operated and the aura of the *éminence grise* on the other side of the door, it was that Declan stopped and lowered his hand.

This was a dilemma. He had something that needed to be seen. That would mean breaking a rule which was more or less carved in stone, but he feared being criticised for having dragged his heels.

Wide awake now, no coffee required, Declan knew that the letter left him with no choice, but here he was weighing up options nonetheless. It appeared the writer was already a client, though Declan did not recognise the scrawl – script would have been too kind a word – and he was instructing 'Stoehlheim and Stoehlheim' to act with immediate effect on his behalf, the word *immediate* underlined with a stroke of jagged intensity. Given the strong possibility that Stoehlheim would not emerge from his office at all that morning, Declan would have to break the taboo and go to him.

Wouldn't he?

He mulled it over and then moved away from the door. Fumbling in another jacket pocket, he found his mobile phone.

His thumb hovered for a seeming eternity over the Emergency Call icon. Hesitant, biting on his lower lip, Declan looked again at Stoehlheim's door. Then he closed his eyes, shook his head and returned the phone to his pocket.

Tiptoeing back to his desk, he placed the coffee cup in his drawer, glancing all the time over his shoulder. Now he flicked off his computer again, returned the remaining letters to the post tray, before turning to Edward, whom he was aware had been watching him in astonished bewilderment for the last minutes.

"I wasn't here yet."

With that he left, closing the door softly.

Declan hurried to his car, jumped in.

The engine coughed, but refused to start. What the hell? He glanced at the display – some warning light was on, but he was fucked if he knew what it was all about. Opening the glovebox, he took out the user guide, but the weight of the book, roughly the size of the Old Testament, was enough to see him shove it back. That was the trouble with cars now; you needed a degree in computer technology just to read their minds. Despite repeated attempts, amongst which were scattered liberal helpings of "*COME ON!*" and "*FOR FUCK'S SAKE!*", it wouldn't play ball. All the while, Declan threw anxious looks in the direction of the office windows.

At length, he thumped the steering wheel, got out again and headed back to the building.

He could tell Edward was still pondering the morning's events so far. Now he stared at Declan in confusion as the latter re-entered and crept stealthily to his colleague's desk.

They conversed in whispers.

"Edward, can I use your car? Mine won't start for some reason."

"What the hell for?"

"I left a very important file at home this morning – a statutory declaration for a case this afternoon."

Edward leaned back in his chair. "No way, old chap, I know how you drive."

Declan's tic, that glance towards Stoehlheim's door, kicked in again. "Come on Edward, I'll treat her better than my own mother." He leaned forward, giving a conspiratorial look. "I need the file for a discussion with you know who; if I don't fetch it..."

Edward raised his eyebrows. "Oh boy, you are in the proverbial, my man." He considered. "Okay, but you owe me – big time."

"You think I don't know that?"

Now both of them seemed lost in a few seconds' thought. Then Edward went to hand over the keys, but hesitated. "But what if he sees your car and asks where you are?"

"Just tell him I felt unwell and needed some fresh air. You're a lawyer," he said. "Lie."

There was panic in Edward's eyes. "He'll know."

"Then I'd better get moving." Declan snatched the keys. "He can't see the car from his windows. Besides, I'm not sure he ever opens those curtains."

"He doesn't need to – he sees everything, as well as hears it." Edward considered. "I tell you, if it wasn't for the money and the kudos…"

"All the more reason I need to go. Thanks Edward." He placed a hand on his colleague's shoulder. "Really."

*

Once back outside, he jumped into Edward's Mercedes. Luckily it was a hybrid, so he was able to take off with minimal sound before hitting the main road, putting his foot down…

…and screeching to a halt fifty yards on.

Looking ahead, he could see there had just been a multi-vehicle accident on the highway.

Declan leapt out of the car and hurried down to the junction.

The driver of another car in the queue was speaking on his mobile: "No, I'm going to be late, so push back all the meetings. I don't know!" He was getting impatient with his interlocutor. "Because it's just happened. I'm not sure, but at least three cars and a van. It looks nasty. I can't turn around either, at least not until the police come; it's a one-way street."

Those last words caused Declan to spin around and look back down the road towards his own car and the office – just in time to see a lorry entering at the far end.

"Shit! Shit!"

He sprinted back to the Mercedes, leapt in and reversed at speed. The lorry was looming up and seemed to show no signs of stopping. Declan managed to swerve into the office car park just before the lorry passed.

"Arsehole! I hope you sit there all day now!"

He parked up, killed the engine and then allowed his forehead to slump onto his hands, which were still gripping the wheel.

Once he had recovered, he reached into his pocket and withdrew the letter. He started to read it again, but not before he took in what had just happened. This prompted the most disturbing of thoughts and he found himself looking at the curtained windows at the far end of the building; the gateway to the forbidden world of Sepp Stoehlheim and his mysterious relative.

He read aloud:

"Dear Mr Stoehlheim,

I am writing to confirm my intention to take my own life on this coming Friday 11th December. I believe it is historically a good day to pay debts. Once 10 a.m. has passed, please act with

<u>immediate</u> *effect upon my instructions as discussed and let there be no interference. That being the case, the agreed sum applies.*

In advance, I thank you for your continued services.

Yours sincerely,

Arthur Du Fuss"

Declan puffed out his cheeks and shook his head. Now he looked out through the windscreen to some distant place. "I'm sorry, Mr Du Fuss." He paused. "I tried."

*

Edward looked up as Declan arrived for the third time that morning, then looked at his watch, before saying in a hushed voice: "No way! Even you couldn't have made it in ten minutes."

"You're right – no way. The road was blocked – an accident." He pitched the keys to Edward. "Thank you anyway."

He returned to his seat, sat down with a thump and laid the letter on the desk, pivoting on his chair while he stared at it. Frowning, he stood again and headed across the office towards a large filing cabinet. This he opened and started flicking through the hanging files, watched all the while in bemusement by Edward.

"Du Fuss, Du Fuss, Du Fuss." The name was repeated with each file he pushed aside. "Maybe just Fuss, Fuss…" With a frustrated sweep of the hand he shoved the files back into place. "No Fuss, plenty of bother." He closed the cabinet again, just about remembering not to slam the drawer shut and stepped away empty handed.

"You won't find statutory declarations in there," ventured Edward. "It's a client file."

Declan ignored him, still talking to himself. "No file, no phone number, just the address on the letter. Time to 'fess up, I guess."

"'Fess up? To what?" Edward felt the need to ask, though he had already given up hopes of any salient answers.

Declan re-straightened his tie, twisted his neck as if his collar was a size too small and headed towards Stoehlheim's office, aware his colleague's eyes would be boring into him again from behind. He didn't need to see Edward's fear and doubt – not right now. He folded up the letter again.

"Good luck," said Edward, those two words conveying a dark world of meaning and nuance.

Decision made, Declan moved on, purposeful and resolute for at least a half dozen paces until the floor seemed to turn to sand. Not being a coward by nature, he found his own squeamishness frustrating. These strictures on the efficiency of the office routine were both pedantic and impractical. Yet he had never forgotten the look in Stoehlheim's eyes the first time he had knocked on that door unbidden. The memory of that icy stare still had the power to give him goosebumps. But the urgency of the matter in his hand helped him to summon enough courage to knock. It sounded like a pathetic tap on that solid wooden edifice.

Declan was shaking, and the rush of blood in his ears was so loud he was unsure whether he would hear any response. He stood a while longer, his sense of panic increasing. Then to his astonishment, he heard: "I said enter".

Finding the whole episode faintly surreal, Declan put his palm to his brow and wiped away the sheen of sweat. His hand felt slick on the brass doorknob as he turned it. He tried his best to look assured, but knew that he was failing miserably. However, there was always the chance that Stoehlheim would find it insulting if any member of his staff seemed less than terrified.

Stoehlheim sat at his desk with his fingers tented together. Declan was relieved to find his employer's expression quizzical rather than angry as he stepped into the cool of the office. He guessed that the lawyer always kept his air conditioning running so that he never had to remove his jacket, that badge of authority.

For the longest time, Stoehlheim held him with his eyes as if appraising him, or weighing some facts against each other, while the object of his gaze stood rooted to the spot. Declan made sure that he kept the letter behind his back for now, fearing that it would shake in his trembling hands. When Stoehlheim spoke at last, his voice appeared to rumble from his chest rather than emanate from his mouth. The tone was measured, hypnotic, with a faint Germanic accent.

"So, Mr Donaghue, what matter of import has emboldened you sufficiently to cause you to break one of the cardinal rules of this establishment?" The question appeared open-handed, devoid of the expected menace.

Declan answered, failing to control the trepidation in his voice. "Mr Stoehlheim, I'm incredibly sorry to disturb you, but there is an emergency. I believe that this letter requires your immediate attention. I found myself..." He hesitated. "...caught between..." Embarrassed, he brought the letter into view.

"The devil and the deep blue sea?" ventured Stoehlheim as a possible completion of the sentence. He extended his hand towards the letter.

"Ordinarily, of course, I would not have dared to..." Again, his voice trailed off as he noticed Stoehlheim's hand, the fingers clicking in silence, signalling. He passed over the piece of paper.

As Stoehlheim read it, his face was impassive, a canvas devoid of colour. Declan was simply relieved not to be the focus of those eyes. When he had finished reading, Stoehlheim continued to hold the letter, but looked back at the young man. "You have read all of this?" It was, in effect, a rhetorical question.

"I'm...I'm afraid so."

"Then you can assist me in this matter." Stoehlheim put down the letter, stood up and started to move around the vast walnut acreage of his desk. Declan's momentary relief at his mentor's apparent forgiveness translated at speed into a suppressed shudder, both at the prospect of what might lie ahead and the physical proximity of his forbidding master. He looked into the inquisitorial eyes and tried to stay focussed. "First, Mr Donaghue" – there was the faintest guttural rasp on the final syllable – "I must remind you that you are bound by the rules of attorney-client confidentiality." Stoehlheim moved to the door and gave it a slight nudge. It seemed to slam shut with the momentum of its impressive weight.

Stoehlheim's earlier use of the word 'emboldened' had been appropriate. Declan was bursting with a question, which refused to remain unuttered.

"Yes, Mr Stoehlheim, but..."

Stoehlheim turned, looked at him, seeming to weigh up something. "But?" The monosyllable almost challenged Declan, yet he pushed on.

"Mr Stoehlheim, can't we do something about this?" The cold eyes remained fixed on him, but for the moment the lawyer said nothing. "The letter says 10 a.m. and it's only quarter to eight now. The address is perhaps an hour from here in the rush hour traffic. Couldn't we save this man's life?"

"I thought you already tried – and failed."

Declan gave a silent curse for his own stupidity, looked down and then turned cold, remembering his earlier conversation about their all-seeing master. Now he remembered the accident and tried to think on his feet. "I meant ring the police. I heard there was an accident, so clearly we couldn't go ourselves."

There was a moment of inner disbelief as Declan digested his attempt to spin things. When he looked up again he was taken aback to see the faintest of smiles cross Stoehlheim's lips, almost tinged with approval, before he pursed them.

"Tell me, Mr Donaghue, what precisely could the police do, assuming we were to break our client's confidence in this way?"

"Well," he paused, "if he has a gun, they could take it away from him. Say that the letter proves he is of unsound mind and not fit to have the licence."

Stoehlheim nodded and did not appear perturbed. "It is a fair comment, Mr Donaghue, but first, if a man really wants to die, he will find a way, such as pulling the trigger a bit earlier than planned. Anything else is just a pathetic cry for help. And is there not something to be said for a quick end to an unhappy life?"

"Perhaps this is a cry for help!" Declan remembered himself. "Sir."

"Then the client should have sent his letter to the Samaritans. Let us attend to business."

Stoehlheim gave a dismissive click of his fingers and made to move past his trainee. Declan was fighting to keep a number of emotions in check. Like many a lapsed Catholic, something of his upbringing remained rooted within him, stubborn weeds refusing to die and resisting the best efforts of any Protestant pesticides. "Sir, excuse me, but I'm not sure how good I am going to be at assisting somebody to die."

Now a frisson of emotion did cross Stoehlheim's face, transmuting again at length into something that resembled a half-smile. "Mr Donaghue, you are merely assisting me. Use that sophistry whichever way you like to ease your conscience. This letter represents a client's instructions. You will recall that he reminds us of that. There will be no interference from the authorities. Trust me. At worst we can simply say that we did not receive this letter or open it until this afternoon. Naturally we advised the police of what had happened as soon as we knew, though unfortunately that will have proved to be too late. The instructions do not prevent us from calling the police, but they do specify something else."

The contorted tenses in Stoehlheim's exposition were confusing Declan, but his employer walked past him to a wall safe, which he opened. He removed a bundle of letters, untied them and handed them to the young apprentice.

"So, Mr Donaghue, enough soul searching. At two o'clock this afternoon..." Here he gave Declan a meaningful look. "... which is of course the time at which we opened the letter from Mister Du Fuss, please contact the relevant constabulary and inform them of this potential tragic incident. Before that, you will have delivered these letters by hand."

Declan flicked through the envelopes and noticed with surprise that they were all in the same road. Consecutive numbers, except for Number Three, which was missing; the address he now knew was the client's. The thought of walking down that street, knowing that one of the houses contained its owner's dead body made his stomach lurch.

As he looked at the letter for Number Four, the home of Mrs Celia Braddock, he saw Stoehlheim's long, perfectly manicured finger touch the envelope. "This one you must deliver tomorrow morning. I realise that is a Saturday, but rest assured double-time remuneration will apply. Mr Du Fuss gave me that instruction verbally. It was his idea of a joke. I remember the look of satisfaction on his face as he imagined this..." He stopped and clicked his fingers, seeking recall. "...what did he call her, ah yes, this dried-up old witch's frustration at being the last to receive it."

The lawyer responded to Declan's frown of puzzlement with a shrug, but the young man's mind was down another track. "Was he here then? I don't remember him, neither face nor name."

"Some arrangements are as old as you are young and sometimes slow-witted, Mr Donaghue. The office of a successful lawyer has no walls."

It appeared that enigmatic statement signalled the end of this audience, for Stoehlheim turned his back on the young man and returned to his seat, making a gesture of dismissal over his shoulder.

Declan was about to step out of the office, but turned when he heard Stoehlheim's voice. "You know, Mr Donaghue, you need to toughen up. I am sure you learnt, for example, just minutes ago, a good liar – and for liar you may read lawyer – needs a good memory. You have the makings of something fine in you, but you will not survive long in this profession if you cannot control your nobler instincts. I have seen them come and go."

"Yes, sir." Declan turned to leave again and was halted in his tracks once more.

"Read again the main paragraph." Stoehlheim held the letter at arm's length and Declan returned to look. "The part where it talks about *the agreed sum*. The detail missing there is a figure, but I assure you a fine sum of money is coming the way of *'Stoehlheim and Stoehlheim'*, a voluntary seven figure contribution from the deceased, the soon to be ex-Mr Du Fuss. Naturally, as my assistant in this matter, your usual five per cent commission will apply."

"Yes, sir. Thank you, sir."

*

The door closed, but not before Stoehlheim saw in Declan's eyes the impact of what he had heard.

Stoehlheim returned to his seat and scanned the letter. He re-read it, again without a trace of emotion. Then he said aloud, "Well, Arthur Du Fuss, do you have the courage? Are you able to keep your word?" He closed his eyes. "I wish I could tell you to rest in peace, but I am afraid I cannot." The dark gift enabled him to see many things. Stoehlheim opened his eyes, put down the letter and, as he looked in the direction of the door, he started to smile, then said to no-one in particular: "Let the game commence."

CHAPTER 4

With a heaving sigh, Arthur moved towards the main bedroom, which he had shared with Helen for twenty years. It should have been thirty-five. He did not go willingly, fearing those memories, which, like so many things you cherished the most, could harm you beyond words. Taking the key from his pocket, he unlocked the door and pushed it open, then entered with great wariness. He shuddered.

"Every time."

He looked around at that spotlessly clean shrine to her memory. He took in the 1980s décor – how she had nagged him to redecorate. Who knew a tin of paint might save a relationship?

"Absurd!"

In the stillness that followed there was chastisement. The anger had no place today.

He stared at the double bed, covered in a peach candle-wick bedspread that blended perfectly with the magnolia walls, chintz curtains and cream shagpile carpet. They had made love there.

Yes, Arthur, they had made love there, taunted the demons.

The marriage had died there.

On that bed lay a black dress, stockings, underwear and a pair of high heels. Tears started to slide down his face as he looked at them.

He moved across to a dressing table on which lay a selection of tins of powder, make-up, bottles of perfume, hairbrushes, all of it part of the great mystery of a woman's rituals. The immaculate presentation and tidiness of it all was as sure a sign as any that he, not she, had been the last to handle them.

Passing a chest of drawers covered in framed photographs of his wife, Arthur reached a wardrobe. Having stood for some time in front of it, as if it were the cursed entrance to a tomb, he opened the doors, which swung, noiseless, on well-oiled hinges. He looked at her clothes hanging there. Now, reaching in, he embraced an armful, burying his face in them. Weeping, he said:

"I can still smell you."

And so he could, in the musty mixture of the Chanel that she had worn and the dust that she had become.

Turning his attention back to the bed, he picked up the dress and hung it again in the wardrobe.

"We won't be needing that anymore."

Likewise, he took the stockings and lingerie, placing them in the chest of drawers.

With all this done, from another drawer he produced a plastic sheet, unfolded it and placed it across the bed. He picked up one of the pictures of Helen and put it on the window sill. Then, returning to the wardrobe, Arthur reached behind the clothes and withdrew a double-barrelled, sawn-off shotgun: a *lupara* 12-gauge hammer gun. Amazing what one could find at a flea market if one knew where to look! He checked it was loaded and leant it against a bedside cabinet.

He couldn't help but stare at the bed and remembered how they looked and sounded...

...the two naked bodies writhing and moaning, he several years younger than her. Her face is visible over the man's shoulder, her eyes closed in ecstasy, mouth open and gasping. Those eyes open and she looks beyond her lover, pupils now dilated in horror rather than pleasure. She shrieks, tries to release herself from beneath the man, scrabbles up the bed – movements the man mistakes for excitement as he remains intent with his mouth, holding her hips firm.

She begs: "Please...I'm so sorry...I'm so sorry...please!"

He squeezed his eyes shut and slumped on the bed, placing a hand where his vision had lain.

"I forgave you that in time – please forgive me this."

He needed to busy himself, master the almost uncontrollable shaking of his hands. Checking again that the gun was loaded, he placed the sawn-off barrels under his chin, as cold and hard as life itself as they pressed against his skin, and he could still feel the intense vibration of his hands down their unforgiving metal. He pulled the trigger, and at that very moment looked across at the picture, at Helen gazing at him. Perhaps he hoped that her presence would give him strength.

*

In that split second before the top of his head disappeared in a crimson nebula, it seemed that Arthur frowned in dismay. Had there been time for him to recognise the last trick that fate had played on him? Did that final flash image burn onto his retinae before the shotgun shells blew them away? That picture of sweet Helen, younger, surrendering willingly to that very well-endowed young man. Was that the last thing Arthur took with him from this world?

Blood and brains spattered the walls and windows. A fine red mist condensed on the shag-pile carpet. In the ensuing silence, the hall clock began to strike.

*

Across the city, Sepp Stoehlheim gave a sharp look up from the file he was reading and on through the walls of his office towards Hell, as his wall clock chimed 10 a.m.

\

CHAPTER 5

Andrew Hansen pushed the shirts backwards and forwards along the rail erratically, waiting for inspiration and finding none. This wasn't the usual shopping trip for him. Yet again he selected one for closer inspection, before shaking his head in frustration. How difficult could it be to pick out a plain white work shirt? From instinct, he glanced now and then at the pretty sales assistant behind the counter, but even she, with her face that sold a thousand shirts, was not really registering with him.

Though he had a twenty-eight year-old romantic's propensity for falling in love and out again, his mind was full of dark thoughts and his testosterone valve, never set permanently to *on,* was, for once, more or less shut. What was it his last virgin queen, Vanessa, had said to him? If he were an ornithologist, he would always be seeking the bird of paradise, while others would settle for the shag. He remembered that his riposte, that he was 'more of a tit man', had saved the moment. Vanessa had laughed despite herself, not stormed out of the house in her thong and bra clutching her clothes to her ample bosom. She had returned, less aggressive in her sexuality, reading his comment as a compliment for her own majestic pair, and they had made love, rather than fucked, enabling him to rise to this particular occasion. Women needed to remember: men could also be misunderstood.

This was Andrew's gift, to charm girls, not needing that journey always to end in his bed, never losing their friendship, just as they never lost hope that one day, they might clamber their way onto that pedestal reserved for his princess. Now he shook his head in frustration. Why was he thinking all this crap when there were serious matters to contemplate and a fair amount of shame to process? The news about old Arthur at Number Three had shocked him. It was only... he stopped and reckoned... Shit! It was over five years ago that the old fella had knocked on his door to thank him for the Christmas card and extend an open invitation to pop over any time for a drink. Just like now, when he had allowed his mind to wander onto sexual trivialities instead of digesting the dreadful news, so he had allowed five years to drift by. It occurred to him that if the old man had died in less dramatic or tragic circumstances, he might have remained unaware of Arthur's passing.

Pushing the shirts to one side with a clatter of irritation, which caused the sales girl to look up, Andrew headed towards the exit, recalling as he did so the impact of walking into the Close the previous day, all set for a chilled weekend, to find Arthur's house sealed off by police tape. The officer on duty had made it clear that he was not at liberty to say anything before divulging that, at this time, the death was not being treated as suspicious. As he walked on, Andrew had looked again at the van at the entrance to the Close. 'Discreet Bio-cleansing Company' had been emblazoned on its side. He had looked up and seen a man in less than discreet white overalls scrubbing at some indelible mark on the window. As he had stopped to look, the policeman had hurried Andrew along again.

That day had had a further twist in store and Andrew now focused once more on the reason for his visit to this upmarket menswear store; his actual purpose for being there in the first place. Gathering himself together, he returned to the shirt section and picked out the right collar size, before turning and heading towards the tie rack. *'Dress code formal, as a mark of respect'* had been the wording on the invitation which he had found upon entering his house, still stunned by events. Andrew did not possess a suit. In the computer industry it was almost frowned upon to wear one, but while he was not going to invest in one just for this mystery function, he could manage a shirt and tie.

As he picked his way through said ties, he became aware of a very shapely undercarriage next to him. He allowed his eyes to wander upwards and his heart became arrhythmic as he beheld the gorgeous Emma Thomas. She was a doll and he had a real thing about her. *So much for men being misunderstood*, he chastised himself. She embodied everything that he looked for in a woman: pretty, toned, yet curvaceous. She worked out at his gym, and so many nights he had gone hard, then soft again, as he imagined sweaty post-workout encounters with her. Darren Thomas was lucky to have at his beck and call this potent brew of a woman, stable in temperament but undoubtedly explosive when shaken.

And here she was, buying her man a tie. Andrew would have loved to come home to her.

Blushing, he spoke: "Hi, Emma." She looked up startled and then, to his delight, gave a big smile.

"Hi Andrew!"

She remembered his name! That constituted base camp at least.

She's married, Andrew!

"That's a nice one you have there," he said, nodding towards the tie in her hand. "That'll suit Darren."

Her face seemed to colour and she looked confused for some reason. "Uh, yeah, I guess. Do you think so?" She held the bold blue and red checked item against her blouse, being a little playful.

"Well, it certainly suits you."

Both of them blushed. "How are you, Andrew?"

His name again. Was she giving some sort of signal? Where did hope stop and desire begin?

"A bit shocked by the news," he replied, grateful that he had a proper topic for discussion, enabling him to hide the glorious discomfort that Emma's presence always induced.

"You mean about Mr Du Fuss? Yes, it's terrible, isn't it? I feel so guilty that I never made the effort to get to know him." She looked away with a wistful expression. "Now I can only imagine how lonely he must have been."

"Yes, I'm in the same boat." He decided that boat needed a slight change of tack. "I was home early yesterday. It was bad enough seeing the van at the top of the Close and then I remembered his wife supposedly died of a horrible disease some years ago, so I just hope it wasn't the same for him. I thought I'd spare myself the gory details when I saw Celia Braddock hovering around, so I pretended to be on the phone and got past her, but she seemed to be trying to nose around and just ignored me."

"Oh, that woman!" Emma pursed her lips. Her lilting Welsh accent, which grew more pronounced when she was angry, broke the last word into emphatic syllables.

"The eye of Sauron," said Andrew. Emma looked blank. "From 'The Lord of the Rings'."

"Oh, um, I've seen the film with Darren."

"Well, you remember that big eye that saw everything?"

"Yes, yes, you're right. That's her!" She placed a companionable hand on his arm and he continued to try to focus. Feeling a supreme, wonderful awkwardness, Andrew deemed it unnecessary to repeat the smutty joke that he had told many times to girlfriends, about how he dared not slip their ring on his finger in case the dark force opposite should see him. It was inappropriate to the moment and to the ears of the woman in front of him. "Are you breaking the mould then?"

Andrew was lost for a moment until he saw the direction in which Emma was looking. "Oh this," he said, holding up a tie he had selected from the rack.

"Well, I don't think I've ever seen you in one. Personally, I think this one would suit you better," she said, playfully holding the tie in her hand up to Andrew's shirt, "though perhaps not with those checks." He felt a light sweat form on his top lip. "That other one seems too stuffy for you."

"Well, the thing is, I've had this invitation to some sort of a formal function. I don't really know what to buy as it seems it might be taking place in a solicitors' office. It said dress code formal..." He trailed off as he noticed the look on Emma's face. "What's the matter Emma?"

"...as a mark of respect. You too? You've had one of those invitations as well?"

"What do you mean?"

"Just that I got this handwritten envelope, or rather we got it, containing an invitation to some sort of a ceremony on Monday evening. It said that it could well be..."

"...very beneficial." Now Andrew took up the text. "The reception to be held at the prestigious offices of 'Stoehlheim and Stoehlheim' at..."

"Isn't it strange?!" Emma bit her lip, and there was excitement in her eyes.

"I wonder if I've been sent someone's invitation by mistake," said Andrew. "But no, I can't have. It's got my name at the top of the letter as well as on the envelope."

"I wonder if everyone in the Close has received one."

"Ask Celia Braddock."

His cutting response drew a smile of approval from Emma, but it soon died. "Everyone except poor Mr Du Fuss, of course." It seemed Emma felt ashamed of her excitement. "Well, he may have received one, but he won't be attending." She stopped, tutted. "I'm sorry, that sounds dreadful. Sometimes I should just shut up." Her head snapped up as she sought a diversion. "Anyway, whatever – I still think this tie looks better than that one." She had grabbed a bold number from the rack. "You wouldn't want to be mistaken for a solicitor, now would you?"

She giggled and Andrew laughed. "I will happily take your advice," he said, and replaced his own selection on the rack. "Darren's a lucky man."

Their eyes locked perhaps a second or two longer than necessary. Emma looked awkward, Andrew embarrassed, but the words were out. Time to move on.

"Guess I'll see you Monday," she said.

"Guess so."

She headed to the checkout with the distinctive red and blue tie.

Allowing time for her to pay and leave, Andrew bought his shirt and the tie she had selected, placing it like some treasured artefact into his plastic bag. He glanced around in the hope of giving, or receiving, another wave, but she was walking in the opposite direction. Then he moved on, carrying with him a tie and a deep envy of Darren Thomas.

CHAPTER 6

For Sandra O'Reilly the charge of excitement hung in the air again on that Monday evening like the precursor to a storm, and for that she was grateful.

On the drive home she had still been basking somewhat in the glow of self-satisfaction, in all the manifestations of that last word, following the weekend's conference. Her branch of 'Barford and Whitaker' had won first prize as the top-selling office in the country for that estate agency. After picking up the award at the year-end gala dinner, flushed with pride and a few too many margaritas, she had pulled, big time, in the downtown bar which the hardier of them had visited on that Saturday night.

It had been just the way she liked it: back to his gaff rather than having to sneak anyone through Reception and hoping you avoided colleagues; no questions, no holds or indeed holes barred; and when it was over, all she had surrendered to him – to them in fact, as his wife decided she wanted to be included! – was one of those mock business cards. She giggled. She had never bothered to check whether the pseudonym belonged to someone. Almost certainly it did. Although the business number given was phony, she had to laugh as she imagined a Madeleine Washington somewhere having her peace disturbed by a horny would-be lover or two at her front door looking to relive old times. The look on all parties' faces would be something to see.

What was important to her – always – was that her home remained her castle. There was no lover to soil her bed by being there in the morning, or to break any of her precious *objets d'art*.

Now she frowned. When she had entered her house a few minutes ago, dropping her case and various folders and then picking up the post, she had headed as always into the lounge. She had chucked the letters onto a table, poured a large whisky and lit a cigarette. Kicking off her shoes, she then walked around the room, pausing at shelf after shelf of porcelain figures.

"Hello my lovelies."

But she couldn't help it – had felt compelled as ever to return to the Cinderella display and stare at the awful gap where the glass coach should have been. Angry tears had filled her eyes, as they did now once again remembering it. Who had done this to her? Her happiness would never be complete unless she found out what had happened to that last purchase. Sometimes she hated herself for the shallowness that allowed someone the power to do that to her. Each time she had come home of late, she had been aware of the piece missing from the ornamental portrayal of her life.

She had taken another large swig of whisky, the smell of which, given her state of mind, brought sudden unpleasant memories of its own, and turned to the post. Luckily, she had gone straight from the hotel to the office that morning, so there had been a pile of letters on her doormat when she got home, a welcome distraction to stop her fretting. It was just as well that she had flicked through it sooner rather than later, because the handwritten envelope had caught her eye.

She had opened it and read, turned it over for any further clues, but found nothing. Glancing at her watch, she had contemplated for a moment and then dashed upstairs, leaving the rest of the mail unopened.

*

And here she was, changed into a dark suit with a skirt well above the knee. She pinned a platinum brooch to her lapel before spraying plenty of Elizabeth Arden perfume on her neck, cleavage and clothes. She checked her teeth in the mirror, plumped her bust, smoothed her hair and dashed out.

*

As she drove along, Sandra kept glancing at the invitation, which lay now on the passenger seat of her classic Audi TT. Rain was falling with increasing spite so she tried to focus on the road, not least because only now had she remembered those large swigs of whisky! At length she had to stop at a red light. She picked up the invitation and tapped it a few times on the leather steering wheel, full of thought, before resting it there and reading the words out loud again: "You are cordially invited to a surprise unveiling at the prestigious city centre offices of '*Stoehlheim and Stoehlheim*', 2–4 Grove Mews etcetera, etcetera. Your presence is important to us, so we do hope that you will be able to attend. The main event of the evening may prove to be extremely beneficial to you. Time 8 p.m. Dress code formal, as a mark of respect." She glanced at the expanse of stockinged thighs she was showing; she had always loved the way a well-lined skirt had a propensity to slide up as you sat. There was more than one way of ensuring the attention of visitors to your award-winning estate agency offices! Who knew whether her outfit might not help this evening to turn out as beneficial as the invitation suggested? Besides, couldn't *formal* make certain things a formality?

A sudden boom of thunder made her jump from the path of her thoughts. Sandra cast a childlike, fearful glance up at the sky. She had given fleeting consideration while getting ready as to whether there was a chance that this was a hoax, or that there might be some danger involved, and that almost symbolic peal of thunder had been timed to perfection. Had some jealous ex-lay of hers tracked her down? However, a quick check on Google before setting off had confirmed that the invitation came from a reputable company, a law firm in an uptown location. Then she had cast all prevarication aside. She'd had just ninety minutes from opening the letter to making the appointment on time. For whatever reason, she had felt compelled to attend.

Once again, as if symbolism reigned, the lights changed to green and she moved on.

The rain was hammering; the windscreen wipers were working overtime to clear the torrents. She drove with care, peering through curtains of water. Spotting a narrow opening on the left that seemed to match the Waze instructions – her classic car didn't have a built-in satnav and she was reliant on her phone – she signalled and turned.

Excitement was mounting. She didn't travel into the city centre very often and as those trips usually involved some event to which she was looking forward, whether a play, a gig, or better still a liaison with a latest or future conquest, the sense of anticipation now was almost Pavlovian.

In the dark dampness of Grove Mews, she was pleased to see there were parking spaces allocated to 'Stoehlheim and Stoehlheim'. Most of them were occupied. On instinct she was glad that she was not alone. There were lights on in the offices, but the road was not well-lit. It seemed the local council was opting for a Victorian gaslight feel to promote a sense of *olde worlde* charm, but the only image this prompted for her was Jack the Ripper.

The Audi squelched to a halt in one of the parking slots. Sandra got out holding a raincoat over her head. She glanced at her watch – it showed 7.55. Hurrying through the car park, casting nervous glances around her, stiletto heels scraping on the pavement, she splashed her way to the door of 'Stoehlheim and Stoehlheim' and rang the bell. While she waited under the cover of the porch, she straightened her suit. Such was the random mischievousness of the human mind in some moments of apprehension, she found herself smiling at the little ritual that involved tugging downwards on the hem of a skirt, which had been selected to show off the maximum amount of leg.

After a short eternity of waiting, the door was opened by a tall, well-groomed, impeccably dressed man who, though seeming to be in his sixties, perhaps older, exuded physical strength. Even the steel-grey hair, which he had swept back though receding at the temples, was thick and plentiful.

Dracula! This was Castle Dracula!

The thought came with such swiftness, she hoped she had not blurted it out. If she had, the gentleman appeared to be sparing her blushes, because he smiled and gestured for her to enter, taking from her the soaking raincoat as he spoke: "A foul night. Fair is foul and foul is fair. Welcome, Miss O'Reilly."

He took her hand in his hot, dry one – a surprise, as he had been holding the raincoat. He had an accent, which may as well have been Transylvanian, and Sandra was glad that she could transmute her smirk into a puzzled smile.

The man seemed to read her expression as she had hoped. "Oh, it's no magic trick – I know who you are because you are the last to arrive. But as a necessary precaution, I would ask that you show me the invitation." He extended a hand in anticipation.

Sandra made to open her handbag and then tutted in irritation. "I'm sorry – I left it on the seat of the car. But, hey, I wouldn't be here if I hadn't..."

"My apologies, Miss O'Reilly, but I must insist. No disrespect intended, just a necessary precaution. I may know your name, but not you. You could be a friend in whom Miss O'Reilly confided. I realise the letter will not disprove that, but still..."

He wasn't backing down, or standing aside. "I understand. Bear with me a minute."

He handed her the raincoat again and she nipped back to the car, returning with the invitation. She handed it over, he ran his eye across it and looked at her. For a moment, as their eyes met, she could have sworn there was some hint of recognition from him, but he said:

"Thank you for your understanding. Please go through. The others are already in the anteroom. Please join them for a sherry."

At first Sandra frowned. "The others...? Ah!" The penny dropped. "I meant to ask – you said last to arrive." As she spoke, she looked down the hallway towards the door from which a murmur of voices emanated, but Stoehlheim gave no response, simply extending his arm in the relevant direction.

She headed that way, but then looked back – Stoehlheim had already disappeared. Grinning, this time she said it under her breath: "Castle Dracula!"

She entered the room and the conversation stopped dead, as did she in her tracks. She scanned the guests. They were all here, all the residents of Merryking Close: Brad Llewellyn, that old bitch Celia Braddock, Darren and Emma Thomas, young Andrew Thingummy and Yvonne Elmer. Her pulse lurched a little at the sight of the elegantly clad lawyer. But there was someone missing, wasn't there? Old Whatsisname from next door. But then she wouldn't have known if the old git were dead or alive.

Emma from across the road was the first one to approach her, breaking away from the huddle to make her feel more welcome. "Hi. Can't say it's much of a surprise to see you."

There was some muted laughter from the others, though it struck Sandra as being a tad nervous.

Andrew Thingummy had moved across to a drinks tray on the sideboard and poured a sherry. He brought it across, handed it over and Sandra thanked him – no hint of flirtation; he wasn't her sort in many ways, one of them being that he knew where she lived! She was about to ask him a question, but he pre-empted it with his next words: "Before you ask, no, none of us has got any idea what this is all about, but it seems that we've all received the same invitation and are all curious enough to have turned up. Except for poor old Mr Du Fuss, of course." Sandra gave him a quizzical look at first, but then said: "Oh, is that the creep's name?"

Celia Braddock gave a snort of derision and said, with all her customary malice: "That just about says it all. Even one of his immediate next-door neighbours didn't know his name. All he ever cared about was what he could peep at through his curtains."

All of a sudden, everybody seemed to find his or her feet fascinating. Some looked in distaste at Celia and Emma muttered under her breath: "Pot, kettle, black."

"Well, I must admit there have been times when I think I've caught him watching me…" Sandra paused. "Hold on… *didn't know…cared about…*what's with the past tense?" She felt a sudden chill.

Now Brad Llewellyn, who had wandered across, chipped in. "Didn't you know that either? He doesn't care about much anymore."

"What do you mean?" The question was more or less pointless. She thought she knew what was coming; could almost read it in the faces around her.

Brad, who was slurring a little said: "Poor bastard topped himself last Friday."

Sandra stared at him and he winked back, a gesture causing her all the discomfort she presumed he hoped it would. Gathering herself together she said: "Oh, that's terrible! How? I mean, I've been away for the weekend. I only picked up this invitation when I got in this evening." She blanched and was grateful that she had not expressed in full her earlier thoughts, because she had been about to agree with Celia Braddock about her ex-neighbour – a unique occurrence. That very Friday morning last, she could have sworn he was peering at her from his lounge window and there had been other occasions when she had been sunbathing or had nipped outside in her nightie. Not someone given to shame, she found herself now regretting the last words she had mouthed to the old…man.

Anyway, on reflection, the observation was a bit rich coming from Celia Braddock, so she was grateful she had stopped herself. She pushed on. "I saw nothing untoward. What happened?"

"They had the house taped off on Friday, but they seem satisfied that it was straightforward suicide," said Brad. "He decided to decorate his bedroom a shade known as grey matter."

Brad mimed a gun to the temple with his fingers. Sandra took a nervous sip of her sherry.

Emma Thomas winced and looked a little pale. "Oh really, Brad!"

Sandra noticed how from Emma's mouth, that telling-off sounded almost a little indulgent.

Now Emma was addressing Andrew Hansen. "We were only saying on Saturday, weren't we, how awful it was and that it showed how lonely he must have been."

Sandra turned from conjecturing about Emma and Brad to observing the way Darren Thomas' gaze was flicking between his wife and Andrew as he asked: "When on Saturday?"

His question, which carried a certain edge, went unanswered, perhaps unheard, as Andrew spoke up. "I sent him a Christmas card the first year I moved into the Close, posted one to all of you." They all nodded. "He came over to thank me and said I must pop in for a drink sometime. I meant to." The lad looked crestfallen. "Now it's too late. What was it John Lennon said about life?"

His rhetorical question was answered by Yvonne Elmer, who spoke up for the first time. "It's what happens to us while we're busy making other plans."

Everyone turned to look at her, though perhaps not with the same intensity as Sandra. When their eyes met, Yvonne took a quick sip of her drink, as if to break the contact.

Sandra got back on track. "Who was the lucky person who found him?"

Brad chuckled. "Who, John Lennon?" He swaggered away from the group towards the sherry. "John Lennon, hah." He repeated the name of the murdered Beatle under his breath, very taken with his own perceived quick-wittedness.

Yvonne watched him with evident distaste before saying: "Apparently the police were tipped off by a firm of solicitors, ironically enough," she said, with a gesture towards the building around them, "who received a letter from Mr Du Fuss advising them of his intentions on the very day he took his life. They called the police, but it was too late."

Emma gave a visible shudder. "Isn't that crazy?"

"Well so was he, evidently," snorted Celia.

Yvonne ignored her and continued: "The really crazy part was that they are executors of his will apparently."

"Executors," said Brad, giggling as he returned, emphasising the first syllable to give the word a different inflection, before asking Yvonne: "And you know this how?"

She lifted her head with an air of superiority that Sandra found both distasteful and enviable. "Well as I was the first to arrive this evening – I don't work far from here – Stoehlheim and I talked, as lawyers do."

Just then, her phone chirruped with a text message alert. She took it from her bag, looked, and excused herself, wandering away from the others while dialling a number.

*

Andrew Hansen had become fixated by a piece of clothing from the moment he noticed Brad Llewellyn straightening his tie. There had been something about the playboy from the outset and now he'd nailed it. His tie was almost identical to the one that Emma Thomas had chosen for her husband in the men's outfitters on Saturday. He wondered if Emma had noticed and watched her for a minute or two, hoping to catch her eye, but she appeared to have eyes for no man in the room, not even for her husband.

Now he clocked how Darren was approaching his wife with a certain steeliness in his eye. He watched how he took her by the elbow and led her across the room. Though he couldn't hear them, he could see the caged anger in their exchange.

*

Darren strained to keep his words hushed: "What were you doing meeting up with Andrew Hansen on Saturday? You never told me."

Emma gave a pointed look down at his hand, but he held her tight. "What? Oh don't start with your stupid accusations again!"

"So why didn't you tell me?"

"There's nothing to tell. I bumped into him when he was looking at clothes."

"Does he often look in the women's section?"

70

"I was in the men's section – looking for something for *you* actually."

She yanked her arm away from him and then turned, heading back towards the others with a fixed smile on her face. Making straight for Andrew, she said in a voice loud enough for Darren to hear: "I told you it would suit you." She ran her hand down the tie.

Darren saw Andrew blush as he looked past Emma's shoulder and straight at him – a look he returned with dark interest. Emma still had her hand on Andrew's chest. Why did she do these things? Was he, Darren, in some way to blame? Was he being jealous for no reason, causing a *damned if I do, damned if I don't* mindset where she then aimed to pay him back?

Not for the first time, he cursed his enslavement to her body.

*

Sandra wandered over to Yvonne, who was on the phone but straight away looked uncomfortable. When Sandra made it clear she wasn't about to retreat, Yvonne said into her mobile: "Look, I'll call you back later, okay?"

She gave an awkward smile to Sandra, who returned it with a knowing one and said: "This must be a bit of a busman's holiday for you, having to be in the city of an evening – and in a solicitor's office."

"Well, I usually end up working late and grabbing a café supper." "Or something else." Sandra winked and noted how Yvonne was unable to hide her discomfort.

Sandra cast an envious glance at the perfect coiffure and couture of the other woman. She doubted that she herself looked that good, despite her quick shower and change of clothes. What an annoying, sexy bitch.

She continued: "At least it meant you didn't have to change, unlike me. It was all a bit of a rush." With her eyes she invited Yvonne to look her up and down.

"That looks fine...um, very nice."

"You're looking great." She couldn't help herself. "Really sexy." She gave Yvonne another very obvious once over and reached towards her breast. Yvonne tensed, straightened and backed away a bit. "Easy, tiger!" Sandra swept her hand across Yvonne's lapel, brushing away some speck of dirt, real or imaginary. "You know, I can't help feeling a sense of..." She paused for effect. "...anticipation when I head into the city for the evening. You never know when you'll have an exciting assignation. I guess I can't switch off the estate agent in me." She paused again. "This is the bedroom." She mimicked her practised gesture.

Yvonne started to move away, but Sandra continued: "For what it's worth..." Yvonne stopped, but without looking round. "...my door is always open...and so am I. You remember?"

Now Yvonne did turn. "Mine isn't." She glanced at the others, who seemed in their own distracted conversations for the moment, stepped closer to Sandra and said: "Didn't our confirmed bachelor playboy buy Number Six from you?" She gestured with a slight inclination of the head towards

Brad. "Rumour has it, he got more than he bargained for there – and so did you."

Sandra glanced across at Brad, who was checking his mobile phone. She became aware of some emotion, a hybrid of anger and sadness, crossing her features.

With a sardonic grin, Yvonne wandered away.

*

If ever there were proof definitive that women held all the weapons in the battle of the sexes, particularly relating to younger male soldiers, Andrew could feel it now in the way his heart thundered as Emma stood in front of him, running her hand down the length of the tie.

"Yes, thank you," he stuttered. "You chose well." He lowered his voice. "Talking of ties, did you notice Brad's?"

Strange that Emma now flushed and raised her hand to stop him. Andrew became aware that Darren, who was moving towards them, might have been listening as his head tilted to one side and there was a look of puzzlement on his features.

*

Everything, latent or substantive, stopped when a door opened at the far end of the room and in walked the tall, steel-haired gentleman who had admitted them all to the building. As he spoke, his voice seemed to flow into their ears and his presence filled the space around him. Though Andrew knew it was only a trick of the light, it seemed the man's shadow moved for a split second after he stopped.

"Ladies and gentlemen, good evening again. You are more than welcome to the offices of 'Stoehlheim and Stoehlheim'. My name is Sepp Stoehlheim and, to use a showtime cliché, I am your host for the evening." He smiled. "I am sure that tonight will be full of surprises for you, and for one of you it will, I hope, be a particularly pleasant one."

Brad Llewellyn was the first to speak. "Could you tell us exactly what…"

Stoehlheim raised his hand to cut him off. "Mr Llewellyn, I can assure that all will be revealed, and soon. Did the invitation not state that this would be an unveiling? A surprise that is revealed in advance is a contradiction, not a surprise. I beg you, please refill your sherry glasses and then follow me through this door." He turned, paused, turned back and pointed to a table by the door. "Oh and please would you be kind enough to leave your mobile phones here." Andrew observed how everyone exchanged uncertain glances and that this was not lost on Stoehlheim, who gave the merest of ironic smiles. "I assure you they will be here when you return and you will be able to live again. I am simply following a request for absolute confidentiality."

Everyone did as bidden, but only Brad Llewellyn took the time to fill his glass before hurrying after the others who had followed their mesmeric host almost with obedience into what appeared to be a boardroom. Down the middle ran a large, highly polished oak table. On this was a covered object. The windows of the corridor between the rooms were shuttered and the rain could be heard thrashing against them, followed by a distant rumble of thunder. The boardroom oozed wealth; it was cavernous, oak-panelled. Cases of leather-bound books covered the walls and shimmering decanters stood on a gleaming tray on the sideboard alongside boxes of cigars. The floor was glinting parquet beneath a central Turkish rug. There was a curious scent combination of expensive aftershave, Cuban cigars, rich fabric and high-quality leather. The lighting was subdued, emanating from up-lighters on the walls.

Emma pulled her jacket closer around her and whispered "Cold" to no-one in particular.

"Like the heart of a liar," said Stoehlheim. He was some distance from her when he responded and Emma was startled.

Having seen them all in, Stoehlheim closed the door and all sound of the storm ceased.

There was only one painting in the room, which looked to be a Breughel. Andrew wandered over to it, studied it, while Stoehlheim came and stood behind him, observing.

"The Triumph of Death," said Andrew.

Stoehlheim gave an approving nod. "Indeed."

"Is it original?"

"As sin. I am impressed."

Andrew blushed a little and couldn't help but enjoy the praise. "I heard about it once in a documentary about the events surrounding the Spanish Armada."

Stoehlheim pointed to the army of skeletons. "The artist foreshadows the atrocities committed by the Spanish in the Netherlands."

Now the host turned to the other guests and gestured. "Please – sit."

All eyes were drawn to the large object at one end of the main table, covered in a damask sheet. There were seven chairs clustered around it.

"Interesting chair count," said Yvonne, a pointed look directed at Stoehlheim as he continued to bid them with a courteous gesture of the palm to their seats.

Now it dawned on Andrew what she meant. Stoehlheim had never queried that Arthur hadn't come along that evening and it was evident he had never been expected. As he started adding things up, it wasn't just the room that cooled his blood, but the slight chill of conjecture. If seven was the answer, two plus two couldn't be the sum. What exactly was going on?

*

Stoehlheim moved towards a seat at the far end of the table, cast in shadow compared with the others. He sat and produced from a leather folder a document printed on watermarked paper. Waiting until the veiled object no longer distracted the guests, and when he was sure he had their full attention, when absolute silence had fallen, the lawyer looked at each of them in turn. As his finer senses detected the varied reactions to the situation, he had to hide his amusement. The full gamut of emotions was present, from anticipation to aggression, each with nervousness at its core. He loved having the power to provoke such responses.

The hush was now such that, even to his own ears, his voice seemed to shatter it when he spoke again.

"Ladies and gentlemen, thank you for accepting the invitation to come here tonight. I will waste no more of your soon-to-be valuable time." He allowed himself a smile of self-congratulation at his private joke. "What I have here is a document containing the last wishes of your erstwhile neighbour, Arthur Du Fuss; a makeshift will, if you like, though perfectly legal."

There were astonished glances around the table – everyone looked at everyone else.

Yvonne seemed annoyed. She caught Stoehlheim's eye and gave a look bordering on accusatory. "So – it was your firm that contacted the police. That explains the chair count, of course."

He looked her straight in the eye. "It seems even in this incestuous profession of ours, Miss Elmer, there are secrets, which can be kept…" he paused, "…where there's a will." He brandished the piece of paper he was holding and gave an ironic grin to emphasise the aged pun. "There are reasons I could not share this information with you, as you will see. Probably none of you know that Mr Du Fuss was a very…" again he paused for effect, "…very wealthy man." The tincture of the nervousness changed; the singular lack of response was proof enough. "Prior to his tragic demise, he had accumulated a twelve million-pound fortune."

Now there was a communal intake of breath, accompanied by the almost audible clicking of cranial calculators.

"You have our attention," said Brad. His eyes were alight with greed. "The crafty old bastard!"

Now there seemed to be the slightest of flickers from the lights, causing everyone to look up and around them. Like schoolchildren who knew someone had just said exactly the wrong thing to the strictest teacher, everyone looked down again at their hands. Darren seemed to be staring at Emma, watching her obvious tension. Stoehlheim looked long at Brad until the latter felt that his collar was a size too small. "More sherry, Mr Llewellyn?"

No response was expected or given.

"Yes, my client was indeed a surprise package. He amassed his fortune through the success of a single enterprise, one that is probably well known to all of you. He was the inventor, perhaps better put, the creator of Chancery."

Everyone looked up and around at each other. No one spoke, but a whisper seemed to hang in the air. Chancery was one of those board games that had become a cult. Like Cluedo or Monopoly, it had sold in millions. Unlike both those games, it had been affected by the political correctness of the later twentieth and early twenty-first century, with the result that its popularity had faded in terms of sales, but intensified amongst its followers, who almost relished being driven underground. It was akin to a board version of 'truth or dare', but more sinister.

"I can see from your faces," continued Stoehlheim, "that the name still means something to some of you."

Yvonne spoke up: "Yes – something to be avoided."

Now Andrew chipped in. "Oh come on, Yvonne, don't be a spoilsport."

"Things are withdrawn from public circulation for a reason," she retorted.

"Yes, by lawyers like you," sniped Brad. "That only whets people's appetites."

"If I may resume," said Stoehlheim with some impatience. "But indeed you are right, Mr Llewellyn. Forbidden fruits have always been mankind's downfall." For a moment he became lost in a memory, one that caused a smile before he continued. "Well, Mr Du Fuss grew rich tapping into the macabre, voyeuristic vein in all of us; our insatiable desire to know each other's darkest secrets and our inability to tell the truth." He gestured towards the covered object.

Stoehlheim stood again. As he did so, he knew his features would be darkened by the shadows. He moved slowly behind the guests as he spoke and there was an edginess emanating from each of them that gave him pleasure, manifesting itself in some as goosebumps on the backs of their necks. "Before we continue, I would ask that you sign this." He brandished another piece of paper.

"And what might that be?" It was Yvonne.

Stoehlheim turned to her. "A non-disclosure agreement. I am about to reveal something, details of which must not leave this room."

He handed it to Yvonne, who read through the single page while everyone waited with ill-masked impatience. When she was done, she gave an almost dismissive shrug and said: "It's brief. There is a lack of details, but likewise nothing for any of you to worry about if you sign it."

"I would just add that failure to sign means this evening stops, for non-signatories, right now." Stoehlheim's tone brooked no argument, but he knew human nature well enough. They would all sign. They were too far in.

Duly, they did. Stoehlheim observed with mixed emotions. Such easy prey – how he wished sometimes for some unpredictability; a rival worthy of crushing.

Now he leaned across and, like a practised Master of Ceremonies, he whipped away the white sheet. "Ladies and gentlemen, back by unpopular demand, I give you Chancery."

There were gasps at the appearance of the object, while mini-spotlights above the table came on, causing it to glint; a huge, circular, marble board with an inlaid seven-pointed star of mother-of-pearl. In its centre was a gold cage. Between the points of the star, visible only from certain angles, were faint faces, rather like holograms, hiding in the dark marble. Engraved in that same marble was a hand-print, one for each player.

Next to the board lay the box lid with the name *Chancery* in gold copperplate. Underneath it, in blood-red italics, from which little droplets seemed to spill, were the words *Do you dare to stand trial?*

"My goodness!" said Emma, "What is that?"

"Jeez, will you look at that!" said Brad.

"What the hell is it?" said Sandra.

Andrew, though awestruck, was grinning. "Never heard of Chancery? I'm the youngest here and I have."

Stoehlheim could tell that Yvonne Elmer in particular was nervous and her question backed this up: "What's this about, Mr Stoehlheim?"

"You might call that the sixty-four thousand dollar question, except that figure will be put in the shade." He gestured towards the board. "And this, despite the adaptations from the original board, is, of course, a game where you cannot lie."

Sandra decided to speak up. "It means nothing to me, so I haven't a clue what adaptations there are. What the hell is this?"

Yvonne, catching a look from Stoehlheim, explained. "It was a game for up to eight players," she looked around at everyone, "on reflection an interesting number, given how many people live, or should I say lived, in Merryking Close and the fact that this board seems set for seven. It took its name from the infamous court in London immortalised by Charles Dickens in Bleak House.

"You could pick one of three figures, meant to represent prisoners awaiting...judgement, to put in the centre of the board. The players' pieces could move towards the centre of the board in stages, dependent upon how truthfully they answered certain questions. If any pieces made it to the centre of the board, the prisoner went free. If two lies were told, he was..." She paused, "...executed." She pointed to the centre of the board, a look of distaste on her face. "In the middle of the normal board there would be the figure of a judge with gavel raised and a caged prisoner in one of three situations, these being on the guillotine, on the scaffold, or in the electric chair. If dishonest answers caused two backward movements of any pieces, another switch was triggered and – the part that appealed to people so much that they would often lie deliberately – the judge's gavel would fall, condemning the prisoner to execution."

At this point she fell silent, but Stoehlheim wasn't done. People needed to feel, to understand the potential horrific consequences of their actions. To know that there would always be a price to pay. He continued: "I am sure some of you remember, with no prompting from me, how the blade would fall and the head would roll from the block, or the body jerk as it fell through the scaffold trapdoor, or the chair glow."

Celia Braddock spoke up now, her words laced with heavy sarcasm. "Fascinating. Is there any chance we could get on with this?

"Indeed," said Stoehlheim, "let us move on to the reason for your presence here tonight. As I said, Mr Du Fuss grew rich from our darker longings. If you remember, what determined whether one's counter moved forwards or backwards were the hand-prints, which reacted to neural and heat signals from our palms and fingers by changing colour. Green signified the truth and red a lie. I have handled high profile divorce cases where the damning evidence was deemed to be that read from a Chancery board." He laughed. "I know of at least one police station where the hand-prints are still used to intimidate suspects in a back room."

Stoehlheim returned to the far end of the table and leaned forward on his own hands. "Certainly the most macabre thing of all is that Mr Du Fuss could think of nothing to do with his fortune once he had made it, perhaps because the success of his venture coincided with the unfortunate death of his wife. He seemed to lose his lust for life."

"If he ever had one." Celia couldn't resist a dig.

Stoehlheim stood and seemed to have grown to an immense height. With a sweep of the hand he said: "Which brings me to you and your presence here tonight." He picked up the will. "Let us contemplate the contents of this document."

No one moved or spoke. They were trying hard to focus through the effects of a cocktail of sherry, adrenalin and ice in their veins.

Now the lawyer gestured towards the ceiling. There was a hiss of static, which was followed by the voice of Arthur Du Fuss. If the guests had been struggling to take in everything until now, that was as nothing compared with this latest shock.

"Dear neighbours, by the time you hear this, I will have taken my leave of this world." Everyone looked up and around in vain for the source of the audio transmission. "It is good to know that I can still make a difference to your lives as you did to mine." The static was growing louder. "It is fifteen years since I lost my beloved Helen. During those years of loneliness, it would have done my heart good to know that there were people to whom I could turn, should it all become too much. Well if you are listening to this, then that point, where it has become too much, has been reached. You know now that I have, or more correctly, had a considerable fortune, which, having no children, I cannot pass down my line. Therefore I feel the money should go to the most deserving person in what was my immediate world. That person will almost certainly be someone capable of winning a final game of Chancery."

"Does he really think he's fooling anybody, the stupid old man?" It was Celia with her usual rather direct and dismissive take on things. "Well I'm not too proud if he wants to squander his fortune like this, and I doubt if anyone else is either."

There was another audible intake of breath around the table, the result of Celia's bluntness, but also because she had been able to make herself heard at all. Assuming Arthur's voice was a recording, why the pause?

Suddenly, the static grew louder. Stoehlheim smiled. If nothing else, though she was an abomination as a person, he had to admire Celia Braddock's forthrightness. He guessed she probably spoke for some of the others too. They were all now leaning forward, straining to hear the rest of Arthur's words.

"If my esteemed servant, Mr Stoehlheim, has followed my instructions, I am sure that you are all now considering your options." Now there was a distinct change of tone. "I am also certain that even the least intelligent of you has worked out that I felt utter contempt for most of you and your black hearts. During the last fifteen years I discovered an eighth mortal sin, that of indifference to your fellow man in his hour of need. Convinced, as I am, that twelve million little maggots have started to eat away the remains of any conscience that some of you may have, I believe I can tell you what I feel. My fortune would have been outweighed, indeed rendered inconsequential by one friendly tap at my front door. So know now, with one exception – and I believe that person knows who he or she is – that whoever wins this money carries away with it my curse. Leaving you with that thought, I will ask Mr Stoehlheim to pause here for a minute, to allow time for anyone who wishes to do so to withdraw."

The word *silence* did not begin to capture the intensity of the soundless void that followed. Five seconds passed; ten. There was movement and everyone turned in expectation. Darren Thomas had shifted slightly in his seat. He apologised to them all with a raised hand.

"Bollocks!" From any other elderly lady that word would have been shocking, but it shot forth with typical anger and contempt from Celia Braddock's mouth. Stoehlheim looked at her with a curious half smile. "Pah, he's just venting his spleen, trying to laugh at us from beyond the grave," she said. "Well, I'm sure he has plenty of company where he is now. Who is he to curse anyway, Mr Big Shot? Thinks he's Tutankhamun, or the Prince of Darkness himself."

"Indeed," the lawyer concurred, an indecipherable something flitting behind his eyes as he did so.

"For once I'm with her," said Brad Llewellyn, bringing a nod from Celia, who then looked askance as the implied insult hit home. "Either bequeath your money to someone or don't. If you want them to have it, don't lay down conditions which you're in no position to impose, especially if no-one asked for your damned inheritance."

"Perhaps a very appropriate turn of phrase," said Stoehlheim, smiling.

Now Darren Thomas took his turn to speak out. "And I tell you what, money may not cure an illness or save a broken marriage, but it can sure make the pain more bearable."

Sandra nodded in agreement. "And anyway, what was to stop him coming and knocking on OUR doors? Not that I'd have let him in, creepy old man – always trying to cop a load of me in my nightie."

"That would be some achievement," said Brad grinning. "Do you own a nightie?"

"What?"

Yvonne turned to Sandra. "I think you might be missing the point."

"Look, don't start getting high-handed with me."

Yvonne placed her hands flat on the table and waited a few seconds before saying "I am simply pointing out that the man was grieving."

"For fifteen years?"

"Yes," Andrew interjected, "it was up to us to put out the hand of friendship. Yvonne's right – we were the majority."

"To be fair to you, you did," said Emma, who leaned across and touched his arm as she spoke. Only Stoehlheim saw the way her husband looked at her. "You sent him a card that first Christmas after you moved in."

*

Andrew's face reddened and not simply because of the gentle yet energising pressure of Emma's fingertips. He looked down, knowing that, while everyone else saw embarrassment, he felt shame that his own hand of friendship had been reached out for, and he had withdrawn it.

He looked at the board in more detail, a version worthy of Las Vegas. He saw again how the star formed by the tracks had seven points instead of the usual eight and that each pointed to one of the prospective players around the table. He remembered how Yvonne had mentioned the chair count earlier. In another departure from the traditional board, there was an open bag of coins in the cage. They looked real enough, glittering in the spotlights of the plush boardroom. Each playing piece was in the shape of a hand, sculpted intricately from something lustrous like obsidian or jet with a fineness and attention to detail. To Andrew, the symbolism was unsubtle – hands reaching for money – and he'd had the unique experience earlier of finding his inner thoughts, or at least the drift of them, being expressed, albeit more crudely, by Celia Braddock.

But for him, the idea of playing the game itself was more compelling than any reward and he knew that he would be unable to get up and walk away from the table now. Arthur's words had caused him great discomfort; Andrew's road to Hell would now always be paved with good intentions. At this moment however, the life and death of Arthur Du Fuss was almost of secondary importance to playing Chancery for real, as it were, with strangers and with a huge prize at stake. How would the others react? What secrets were there to exhume from the compost heaps to which folks had consigned them; people who afterwards would have to continue living cheek by jowl with each other?

He looked at the piles of cards, face down on the board in their respective slots. What mouldering corpses or lost treasures would be disinterred as a result of them? Because what excited and intimidated players of Chancery was not the larger of the two piles, labelled *Little White Lies*, but the smaller pile called *Home Truths*, which could only be answered with *Yes* or *No*. Anyone throwing double six was held to have 'the Devil's luck'; so said the rules in their Gothic script. This person had to take a card from the smaller pile. Many chose to withdraw from the game at this point, which in itself, by inference, was a dangerous ploy. But how much would they dare reveal with millions at stake?

Andrew glanced up to find Stoehlheim looking at him, watching him. How long had he been under observation? The lawyer gave the faintest of smiles and tilted his head, as if he knew something was coming. Stoehlheim waited a little longer. His patience was rewarded when Andrew straightened in his chair and said: "Well I don't know about anybody else, but I can't walk away from this." He extended his hand towards the board. "And I don't mean the fortune – I mean the chance to play. This is a cult game I've never had the opportunity to participate in. For me it would be like digging all the way down to some pharaoh's tomb—"

"Old King Tut," snorted Celia, with a sly glance at Stoehlheim.

"...and then turning away because of a curse on the door. I would be asking myself forever: 'What if?'"

There was not a murmur from anyone. Stoehlheim looked from face to face. "May I take it then that you all intend to play?" Some nodded, some mumbled agreement. Stoehlheim pointed to the little gold cup, which contained two ivory dice. "Then let us have the first victim."

CHAPTER 7

Stoehlheim had laughed after his use of the word *victim*, but the sound put none of them at ease. It was not meant to. He leaned back in his seat, a brooding, judge-like presence, and the image was particularly appropriate. He was chuckling at the irony. When people around the world played Chancery, as they debated which figure to choose for the condemned prisoner, it seemed to escape the attention of all but the most zealous or evangelistic that they were the ones on trial.

Stoehlheim had not bothered to fulfil the last line of Arthur Du Fuss's letter of instruction, perhaps because he felt it was rather theatrical, but also because he believed the morally ignorant deserved no direction. It had been to read out the tag-line on the box lid of the game: DO YOU DARE TO STAND TRIAL? The lawyer looked out for a moment into the void beyond that room, beyond the periphery of the superficial world inhabited by these hapless, ultimately doomed players, into the cold darkness where Arthur would languish forever. He nodded a silent 'thank you' to that desperate and damned soul for providing him, Sepp Stoehlheim, with this evening's entertainment.

He returned from that void like a sleeper being awakened – someone had pushed back a chair and stood up.

*

Yvonne Elmer scraped back her chair and stood slowly. She liked to think that she was an intelligent woman, a corporate lawyer of fifteen years' experience. As someone who had played Chancery many times, she had been thinking things through. The legal firm where she had done her pupillage had owned an edition of the game. It had become a custom for all the staff to gather around the board with several bottles of wine and play a round or two to celebrate particularly successful cases. She had witnessed the potential for ill feeling, embarrassment or worse. The mood of the players could plummet faster than a hanged man. Inference was everything. Since the *Home Truths* questions could only be answered with 'Yes' or 'No' and never be elaborated upon, rumours could smoulder, non sequitur, nonsensical, no matter. For her at least, this game was also a non-starter. First, there was the situation with the Thomas family. Emma had come to her only weeks before, seeking her advice about marriage guidance counselling. This had not come as a complete surprise – when you lived across the way from Brad Llewellyn, the one thing you were guaranteed was a room with a view! It was not an area in which Yvonne had any expertise and given her own recent history, she was hardly in a position to offer objectivity. Nevertheless, she had listened, given some friendly words of debatable wisdom and a contact name. She knew that the wrong type of question from the – in this instance – very appropriately named *Home Truths* cards could lead to an ethical dilemma. She did not want to go there.

"Mr Stoehlheim, I know that I am outside the time limit, but I no longer wish to participate."

"My dear Miss Elmer, how typical of we lawyers, always observing from the shadows. Is it the *Home Truths* cards that concern you?" He gestured towards the board where the two piles of cards stood in their designated slots. "Have you decided that the requirement to answer yes or no to them might compromise some client-attorney confidentiality?"

Damn him! Was he a mind-reader? Yvonne was used to standing in courtrooms and hearing truths turned into lies or vice versa, and saying nothing, but still she blushed. She became aware of a passing car in the street, the sound muffled, distant, and couldn't recall whether it was the first she had heard that evening.

Yvonne glanced towards Emma, who looked away swiftly. She turned again to Stoehlheim and saw her action had not gone unnoticed. He gave the thinnest smile.

That conundrum with Emma was nothing though compared with her agonising over her brief ill-conceived affair with the voracious, highly sexed Sandra O'Reilly. All facets of the word *dirty*, including some that even a well-read woman like her had not encountered, applied to Yvonne's memories of those crazy weeks; she was by turns a little enthralled, but mostly appalled by what she had done. She had only ever taken an oblique glance at her own bisexuality, finding enough pleasure in men to be able to cling by her fingertips to what she, with her career in mind, was forced to consider as respectability by dint of the number of dinosaurs that inhabited the legal planet. Things were changing, but a further sixty-five million years might still pass!

Sandra had forced her to face her latent desires. 'Face' – now that was an interesting choice of word under the circumstances! How many times had they indulged in what her lover described as 'mouth to muff resuscitation'? It was exactly that sort of earthiness and lack of inhibition that had appealed to Yvonne in the beginning. Even now she was stirred remembering it. Perhaps she could never again deny what she was; indeed, why did she need to? But one night, during a particularly sordid session, she had stopped devouring pussy and become transfixed by the huge, swollen cock, which at that moment was ploughing in and out of Sandra's anus, the hairy testicles brushing her nose as it did so. All of a sudden, Yvonne could not shake the thought of this man walking into her office, or squash club, or local pub and she had to stifle the rising hysteria by plunging her face back where it had come from.

From that day she had made herself scarce, even making a show of inviting men back to her house after dates, hoping that Sandra would see that things were different now. It seemed to work. Sandra was promiscuous, though her many lovers never fouled her own doorstep. Yvonne doubted whether it had been too long before the O'Reilly mouth was grazing in pastures new, though she had enough insight to know she was trying to stifle the voice of her own conscience.

Nevertheless, she had been a little concerned this evening by Sandra's tone, her flirtatiousness a few minutes before. Something in the way Sandra had looked at her, with almost a twinkle in her eye, had left room for interpretation. It was to Yvonne's regret that she had stooped to broaching a topic she knew would cause Sandra pain.

Yvonne wanted to avoid divulging secrets or being betrayed. However, she knew the game had the power to destroy. Given the essence of Chancery, she deemed it sensible to withdraw. She turned to their host, to find he was still observing her. He smiled without radiating any warmth or even a sense that he was surprised. If she could have compared the resultant discomfort with anything, it would have been with standing there naked.

"What a sad indictment of our profession, Miss Elmer." He paused as if considering something. "Very well, you may withdraw from the game..." She nodded her thanks, turned to pick up her bag, but he hadn't finished, "...but you may not leave this room."

Whatever insecurities he might have tapped into, Yvonne did not like being spoken to in this way by Stoehlheim. "I'm sorry?" She felt affronted rather than afraid and was power-less to prevent her hands moving to rest on her hips.

Stoehlheim, in turn, raised his own hands defensively, smiled and said: "I do apologise. Even after all these years my English language skills can let me down. I meant that I must ask that you do not leave. It was a request made to me by Mr Du Fuss. He wanted everyone to remain to see that all was done fairly."

"I don't care – I'm leaving. He's dead; what's he going to do about it?"

Now Stoehlheim leaned forward as if conspiratorially, but his words seemed to brook no argument: "Also, he wanted no-one to breathe a word of this night's work until the game was over. No disrespect to you, Miss Elmer, but this session could last for several hours, by which time you could have run to the press, for example, to sell the story."

Yvonne stood her ground. "I signed the NDA."

"You read the document, Miss Elmer – I suspect you noted its lack of clarity. You know therefore that it references and applies to..." He paused to make it clear that he was quoting, "'...*participants in the evening's activities.*' You are a lawyer; given you are withdrawing from the game, you would be well placed to argue the legalities of whether you participated or not."

He was good, she had to give him that, but Yvonne wasn't one for backing down. "I don't need the money. Given, as you say, I am a lawyer, I certainly don't need the publicity." She slung her bag over her shoulder and made to head for the door – at which point, to mix the gaming analogies, Stoehlheim played a trump card.

"Personally I don't think it would reflect well on anybody here if it came to light that they had agreed to gamble in unlicensed premises in the hope of winning a dead stranger's fortune; diced with the Devil, as it were; sold their souls." He paused for effect. "Careers, lives even, can be ruined by such things."

As he spoke, he looked fixedly at Yvonne Elmer. For a moment she returned his gaze. Then she compressed her lips, gave a slow nod acknowledging inevitable defeat and, having moved her chair back from the table, sat down, hoping she looked reluctant, not browbeaten.

Stoehlheim turned to the others. "Now then, shall we continue?"

It seemed that there was the faintest hiss of static, just for a second or two.

*

Andrew reached for the little gold cup and dice, only for Stoehlheim to call a halt.

"To avoid any argument, at least regarding the order of play, Mr Du Fuss has instructed that the order of throwing at the start of each round will always be the door numbers of your addresses. The only variation, as those of you who have played the game will know, follows the throwing of a double six. So," he gestured with an open palm towards Sandra O'Reilly, "as the resident of Number One, perhaps you would be so kind as to set the ball, or rather the dice, rolling."

Sandra looked around and then picked up the cup with the care normally reserved for a communion chalice, never mind one full of potential poison.

*

Brad shook the dice and released them. They rolled across the board and came to a stop. Seven heads craned forward to see the numbers on the ivory cubes.

"Seven," said Emma. She looked at Andrew. "You're top with ten...you first."

Given everyone's apparent willingness – Yvonne excluded – to play the game, it was strange what a sense of relief it seemed to bring not having to go first. Andrew picked that up and it was reinforced by the faces staring at him as he looked around the table. With a shrug of the shoulders he reached across, took a card from the *Little White Lies* pile and then addressed everyone; the other players and Stoehlheim: "So these are the ones we can answer in whatever way – truthfully, of course?" He looked at their host, who nodded. Now he read out loud:

"Have you ever walked away from a situation when your conscience might suggest you should have stayed? If so, give details."

He placed his hand in the time-honoured manner on his designated palm print, which, with a warped sense of humour, Arthur had etched into the surface of a Bible. Adrenaline surged through his body as he spoke: "I was witness to a car accident. As I was late for a lecture, I drove away so that I wouldn't have to get involved, but without checking whether anyone was hurt."

He waited a few seconds and then lifted his hand. The palm print glowed green. Despite knowing that he was telling the truth, he still puffed out his cheeks with relief and went to move his piece one space forward. It moved of its own accord.

There was a gasp around the table. "Very clever," said Andrew to Stoehlheim. He was surprised to see the slightest of frowns darken the lawyer's brow for a moment, as if for once the smooth operator were perplexed by his comment, or found it laced with ambiguity.

From her place set back from the table, Yvonne said: "It's not like any Chancery board I remember. Is it the original one?"

"Oh no," responded Stoehlheim. "Mr Du Fuss made this one especially for tonight; a bespoke version."

Uneasy glances were exchanged around the table at that revelation.

"Hmmm." It was Andrew. "I was thinking earlier about the lack of subtlety in the message here," he gestured towards the board, "those hands all grasping forwards towards the money. We didn't ask to be invited."

"Perhaps you do your potential benefactor discredit," responded Stoehlheim. "Perhaps it is more subtle than you think, though admittedly no less pejorative. Might these be the hands that were never extended in friendship?"

Brad chipped in. "How the hell did...?" He pointed to Andrew's piece, stooped and looked under the table. "No levers or switches I can see."

"Shall we continue?" Stoehlheim interrupted, his impatience conveying the rhetorical nature of the question.

*

They all threw again. In the games of Chancery which had been the making of Arthur's fortune, the top scorer in the last round threw first in the next. Arthur had changed the rules for this tailored board. No-one could argue – as the creator of Chancery, that was his right, even when deceased and besides, no-one was going to take on his lawyer.

This time Sandra top scored with eleven.

"Yessss! My turn!"

Then the implications struck home and she regretted her somewhat crass response.

Emma breathed out shakily. "Be careful what you wish for – I guess." Darren looked across at his wife and said nothing.

Sandra picked up a *Little White Lies* card and read: "Have you ever taken money that wasn't yours to take? If yes, give an example." She was lost in thought, but then seemed to have a revelation. They could all see Sandra's hand shaking as she placed it on the palm print, but she was smiling. "I bought a pair of shoes at Selfridges and was given twenty pounds too much change. I pocketed the change rather than returning it." Again the lifted hand revealed a green palm print. "Yusss!" She gave a fist pump.

Stoehlheim shook his head. "The only hope for mankind is if others see the irony here."

All heads turned towards him. He sat with fingers interwoven and the thinnest, most despairing of smiles. Then they caught sight of Sandra's counter moving forward.

*

And so the game progressed for some time. Everyone had stories to tell of unpaid parking fines, minor theft of goods from supermarket chains and stolen teenage kisses from best friends' partners. The game was moving slowly.

Celia Braddock's patience appeared to be running out as she grabbed the tumbler for her next go. "Oh let's get on with this!" She threw a double six and her parchment skin blanched visibly.

"Devil's luck," said Stoehlheim.

Given the evident discomfort this occurrence seemed to cause to all the players, Stoehlheim had to admire the gallows humour with which Celia responded. "Devil's luck? Ha, if I had been playing with three dice and thrown three sixes, I would have agreed."

"What does that mean – Devil's luck?" asked Emma softly.

Darren responded: "Devil's luck means you have to pick a *Home Truths* card. You can only answer yes or no. Better not to get those, though lying gets you nowhere with either set of cards. It's all in the interpretation."

He held Emma's gaze. She blinked first.

A nervous frisson of fidgeting pulsed through the room. Everyone liked to think it was age that caused Celia's hand to shake as she reached out and took a card from the *Home Truths* pile. Her facial muscles struggled to maintain inscrutability, but she was powerless to prevent the widening of her eyes as she read the card to herself.

Have you ever taken something from someone knowing that it would hurt them deeply? Celia was so mired in her thoughts that she forgot to read out the card and had to be reminded by Stoehlheim.

*

For Celia Braddock, there was no shortage of possible answers, selecting one from the many available. Her problem was, rather, trying to shut out the tapping of the bony hand knocking from inside the cupboard door where she locked her memories.

To her mind, in her defence, he had showered that damned dog with all the love and affection that should have been hers. Of course he had tired of her by then. Hell hath no fury, and it had indeed been a furious blow she had aimed at the beast.

Celia looked around the table, first at Stoehlheim, then at all the others in turn.

She closed her eyes, which only made things worse.

The sound of a dog barking in fear.

Now a wet thud, a whimper, another wet thud.

The splash of something heavy hitting the water. She had forgotten that part, or rather had been successful in locking it away in a tiny room at the back of her mind – that trip down to the canal before he returned home. She had made him a cup of tea. "It happens all the time, Ernest. These dogs from animal homes, they never settle. Look how he's chewed through the lead; how desperate the poor thing was to get away. And it isn't a high fence. Come on now, be a man. Dry those tears."

And into her arms and her bed he had sunk again, mainly for comfort, until she, such is the perversity of love, had tired of him.

So now Celia Braddock was faced with a dilemma. The problem was that whichever path she chose, it would mislead her; there was no correct road and all way-markers pointed to damnation. A pinprick of light remained within the darkness of her soul, which she had never been able to extinguish completely. It was a mere glimmer; not enough to bring salvation or be called a conscience, but sufficient to make her palm print glow an accusatory red.

Thwarted rage twisted her insides. To hell with it, she would try.

She opened her eyes to find everyone looking at her in expectation and not a hint of sympathy in those features. Now she stared straight into the scrutinising face of Sepp Stoehlheim and, for the briefest of moments, saw her own anger reflected there as if he had read her thoughts. He raised his eyebrows, questioning. Celia looked around the table. No other gaze met hers. Now she was the mind-reader who knew what each of *them* was thinking.

She threw the card to one side, placed her hand on her Bible and said a defiant, "No!" Within seconds, not just the hand-print, but the whole Bible burned red – in fact it seemed to pulse, probably casting a devilish glow on her face in the eyes of her pathetic neighbours.

For neither the first nor the last time there was a collective, suppressed gasp around the table as a throb like a heartbeat filled the room. One or two of them overcame their inhibitions long enough to smirk. Sandra O'Reilly drew in a breath, as if she had something to say, but controlled it, though not without evident difficulty.

With a great effort Celia managed to pull her hand away, pushed back her chair and staggered to her feet. She looked at each of them in turn and said: "Your time will come, every one of you."

Now she stared at their host, who smiled and gave what was almost a conspiratorial nod, before responding: "Indubitably. Now please take your seat again. The rules apply to everyone."

"Not to me." She squeezed with impatience past Brad Llewellyn's chair and smirk, making for the door. It was locked. "This is preposterous and an imposition. I demand that you let me go."

The others turned to Stoehlheim. From the looks on their faces it was apparent they were with her on this one – the revelation that the door was locked had spooked them all.

Celia continued her protest: "This is outrageous. Unlock this door!"

Stoehlheim stood, but remained where he was. To all of them he seemed a looming presence in the darkness away from the spotlights.

"Mrs Braddock, twice in one minute you have proved yourself unworthy of trust. Now please be seated," he emphasised each of these last words, "so those more deserving than you might continue with the game. I am sure that everyone here wishes to do so or at least get this game completed in enough time so that they can return to their homes."

Celia was fuming. Nobody could talk to her in this way. She wanted to call the police. She was being held against her will. So no-one was more astonished than her when she returned to her seat without protest. She watched the others pull up their chairs again, almost as unwilling. She knew Stoehlheim had observed their discomfort and his last words had been his way of telling them no-one was going anywhere yet. They too were prisoners of their own greed.

Now Stoehlheim gestured towards the board. They all watched amazed as Celia's piece moved backwards. As she had not yet answered a *Little White Lies* question, her piece simply fell to the floor.

"You will notice," said Stoehlheim, extending his large hand, "that in time-honoured fashion the liar's token has moved back one space. In this liar's case, there was nowhere else to go but out of the game." He looked at Celia, who bridled at the repeated insult, but still held her peace. "As you all know, should this happen twice the entire game is void, and the money, like the soul of Arthur Du Fuss, will remain in Limbo until Judgement Day."

Again there was a slight hiss of static. Fearful heads turned, seeking the sound.

*

Sandra O'Reilly was the exception. Unnoticed by the others during the disturbance of the last few minutes, she had taken Celia's discarded *Home Truths* card, which had landed near her. Now she re-read the wording, before looking at Celia with hatred in her eyes and pocketing the card.

*

They were chilling words, that last comment by the lawyer; for some because of the thought of the wasted millions, but for all of them, to a greater or lesser extent, because of the reminder that they were sitting there gambling for the fortune of a lost soul. Whether you had belief or not, there was something about the eternal judgement on a suicide that raised questions and touched nerves. The idea that someone in such despair that they end their own life might still be punished for eternity – how could it sit easily in any balanced mind? It was like something from a horror movie and the problem was, you didn't get to step out of the cinema afterwards, your darkness lit by the passing cars and the welcoming windows of a pub. Plus you had no proof if you sought to dismiss it. Only in committing the act yourself might you find the truth.

*

Andrew Hansen was contemplating that and much else now, regretting his own stake in Arthur's fate, the guilt of which he could not just shake from his shoulders; someone condemned, if you believed in such things, to an eternity in an empty netherworld. However, seated at this game board now, Andrew felt like Macbeth, having waded halfway across a river of blood, so that turning back was pointless.

He found his focus wandering from this game, which he had been the keenest to play, so it was lucky that more questions about innocent misdemeanours followed. What it meant though, was that he had become more of an objective observer. He saw Emma throw seven and as she uttered the number she looked relieved yet again. Her piece had moved only one square forward and she did not seem to care, making him wonder what dark secrets she was hiding. Given that body and her flirtatiousness, he assumed they would be of a sexual nature. As she was married, that could only lead to trouble.

He regained focus as he heard '*Shit!*' and looked up to find Sandra had thrown double six. Then there was another pulse, an almost imperceptible tide of energy passing through the room. Stoehlheim had been right – truly it was a reflection on humankind, a poor one, if the need to answer simply yes or no could cause such angst. Were people all, by accident or design', duplicitous?

Sandra looked around for moral support, but there was none to be had. Nobody met her gaze. Her clumsy fingers fumbled a *Home Truths* card from the pile at the third attempt. She read: "Have you slept with anybody who is in this room?"

Believing he was the only one truly not playing for the money, Andrew was in many ways appreciating this forum for what it was. He looked around in the silence that followed; saw how all the players avoided eye contact with Sandra. However, with a hint of a smile that surprised him, she said "Yes", having placed a confident hand on her Bible, which immediately glowed green.

Now heads were swivelling. Of course, it was the men who were recipients of furtive or accusatory stares. All of them managed to look guilty and Andrew conjectured whether that was a psychosomatic response from the male of the species, since there were at least two of them who would not have touched Sandra O'Reilly with a forty-foot barge pole.

He saw Emma Thomas look at Darren, who returned her stare with a shrug of the shoulders and a defiant, almost truculent shake of the head. Surely a case of *physician heal thyself*. Andrew was convinced now there was so much more to that saucy minx than met the eye.

He observed how Sandra was looking under her brows at Brad, who in turn was looking at Emma and Darren before he turned to find Miss O'Reilly observing him.

Andrew watched them all, but then had what might have been a Damascene moment. He saw Sandra look in the direction of Yvonne Elmer with a faint smile. Yvonne sat with her eyes downcast. Tiny beads of sweat had broken out on her hairline and on her top lip, which she wiped away now surreptitiously.

None of it mattered for the moment – these were *yes* or *no* cards – but Andrew was sure there would be recriminations. The cat was truly amongst the pigeons and you could almost see the feathers flying.

The tension was snapped by Stoehlheim: "Ladies and gentlemen, the quicker we move on once a truthful answer has been given, the sooner you can all return to your homes..." He paused. "...assuming you wish to."

Andrew suppressed a wry grin. The old lawyer's comment was a reflection of his own thoughts from just moments before.

But indeed, things did need to move on. Andrew's turn came round again, he picked up the cup...and threw another double six, quite against the law of averages. Once again he took a *Home Truths* card, though with less hesitation than before, which surprised him, and read: "Have you ever wronged a neighbour in a way that cannot be put right?"

He gave a shake of the head and smiled, though the latter was a humourless response, full of disbelief.

As one, it seemed the other players grew uneasy and curious as he brandished the card in Stoehlheim's direction, saying: "Something's going on here, isn't it?" The lawyer gave him a non-committal look by way of reply. "Either there's something at work here or this is a big fix."

Stoehlheim raised his hands, palms upwards. "I am afraid you have me at a disadvantage, Mr Hansen. What exactly has been 'fixed'? The intermittent throwing of double sixes; are the dice spectacularly loaded; the order in which random players have picked up cards; is there an imbalance in the questions? I see two possible answers: 'Yes' and 'No', and either one, dependent upon circumstances, would be correct." He brought his hands together, leaning forward out of the shadows. "Or is it rather that some facts and behaviours are universal?"

Andrew allowed his hand to drop, but despite feeling foolish, held his defiant, ironic smile. He placed his hand with an abrupt movement upon his Bible. Looking fixedly at Stoehlheim as he did so, he said a 'Yes'.

*

Most of those around the table were still pondering Stoehlheim's words, but not Darren Thomas, who had reached his own erroneous conclusion. He made a mental note and looked at his wife, at that thick, strawberry blonde hair in which he loved to twist his fingers and pull; at those wonderful breasts, straining the buttons of her blouse, clamouring for release. She shifted in her seat, crossing her legs and the lining of her skirt whispered against her stockings. He knew she was sharing the gifts that should have been his alone, but he had been wrong about the recipient. It was going to be much simpler to eliminate the problem now; much easier to scare off that schoolboy who had wronged him.

*

In the deathly stillness that followed his answer, Andrew caught Darren Thomas looking at Emma's bowed head, his eyes full of anger and jealousy, and understood straight away the misunderstanding that it represented. He lifted his hands in protest, starting to gesture towards Darren.

"STOP!" The barked instruction from Stoehlheim made everyone jump. He pointed at Andrew. "You are fortunate, Mr Hansen that you had lifted your hand from the Bible before you started trying to give an explanation, for you would have broken a cardinal rule of *Home Truths* and that would have been game over."

Andrew looked from Stoehlheim to the palm of his hand and then on to the counter. Even as he watched, it inched forward to the next square.

The green glow of Andrew's hand-print prompted a mixture of curious and accusatory looks. He was one of the good guys; what hope for the rest of them?

*

Another few rounds of questions went by, bringing admissions by the players of venial rather than venal sins and most counters moved forward a space. No-one seemed to notice. The *Home Truths* revelations still hung in the air like dust after an explosion and the remaining pile of cards was another ticking bomb. However, the responses to this probing into inconsequential moral dilemmas found most pieces standing only one or two spaces away from turning their owners' lives upside down. The mist was clearing and the players seemed to regain their focus; their selfish unanimity of purpose.

It came as a fresh shock then, when Brad Llewellyn threw a double six. He paled noticeably.

This was going to be interesting, thought Stoehlheim, and he guessed he knew at least two other people in the room who would echo this sentiment. Brad reached for a card and read – there was an audible click from his throat as he swallowed. He closed his eyes. Everyone else's were on him...

*

...with one exception. Emma Thomas' suppressed gasp had attracted her husband's full attention again. With the rending, dismal satisfaction of a prophet of doom, he watched as she bit her lip. Her ill-concealed agitation intensified as Brad sat deep in thought.

"Care to share, Mr Llewellyn?" It was Stoehlheim.

Brad bit the bullet: "Have you ever had an affair with anyone in this room?"

Darren watched Emma's fingers clasp until the knuckles were white. He could actually see her thumping heartbeat where her breasts pushed against her blouse. Her forehead looked slick and when he looked again at her hands, so were they. So he had been right in his initial fears. It was not Andrew Hansen after all. She was fucking that gelled-up playboy, or maybe she was screwing both of them, perhaps at the same time and her own husband in the process. God knew she loved it enough. And there was that key word – *affair*. He closed his eyes, trying to shut out some of the images that flashed up before them, but they merely projected onto his eyelids. When he opened them again, Stoehlheim was watching him. They exchanged a look. Something passed between them.

Something snapped.

But then both were distracted as Brad Llewellyn leaned forward with an abrupt motion, placed his hand on his Bible and said "No." The hand-print turned green. He threw himself back in his chair as if he had received an electric shock.

Emma released a long-suppressed breath. Her hands remained clenched in her lap. None of this escaped Darren's notice. He watched her.

At first, Brad did not have the energy to smile. His reputation was such that the fading green of his hand-print drew some frankly astonished stares.

*

Not least of these came from Sandra O'Reilly. For her there was the little matter of having aborted his child two years before after a cocaine-fuelled night of madness. She wasn't having this. This was a fix. She slapped her palms on the table and pushed herself to her feet.

"What's going on here?"

The others looked on astonished, an open-mouthed mute choir.

Stoehlheim raised his eyebrows. "Please sit down, Miss O'Reilly."

Sandra stood her ground. "No I won't. There is something going on." She pointed at Brad. "You just lied and got away with it."

Brad looked at and through her. "Well then, fair play to me." He had regained his footing and now looked smug. He drained his sherry glass and placed it back on the table with a bang.

Stoehlheim glared at him, but then turned back to Sandra. "Crudely put by Mr Llewellyn, but there, unfortunately, is the reality, Miss O'Reilly. And if you continue in this manner, I will be forced to bar you from the game. The rulebook clearly states, as it always has, that no player may seek to defame the character of another. As they say in business, the board's decision is final."

Sandra was still staring at Brad. She put protective hands across her stomach. "You bastard! You made me...and then you made me..." She choked on her words, before anger took over again. "There's a conspiracy here."

"Enough!" Stoehlheim stood and his shadow loomed on the wall behind him.

"I've not finished!"

"I am afraid you have." The lawyer's eyes told Sandra that she was dismissed and something else told her that it would be better not to debate the issue. Stoehlheim saw that she understood. He smiled at her and his shadow seemed to grow while he looked at her.

Suddenly, Sandra walks around the table and sinks to her knees in front of Stoehlheim. She opens his zipper. He is wearing no underwear and she draws out his cock. It is huge, thick and veined. She looks up at him, towering above her, and wants to choke on him. He nods at her and she takes him into her mouth, sucking greedily on him, trying to open her throat to take his full length, knowing the others are watching in astonishment from the other end of the table. She feels him grow thicker, feels his hand twist in her hair and suddenly his hot seed is spurting into her mouth and she is swallowing it, here, in front of her neighbours, ashamed in her shamelessness, on her knees as she sucks off the old lawyer.

She swayed and put her hands on the table to steady herself; opened her eyes to be met by concerned looks from those around her. Andrew Hansen laid a supportive hand on her arm.

113

"You've gone quite pale," said Emma. "Are you all right? Looked like you were about to faint, you did."

Sandra nodded. "I'm okay, thanks." She looked down the table at Stoehlheim, making sure that her gaze did not stray below his eyes. He smiled. Full of understanding now, she went quiet, compliant, and pushed back her chair before taking her seat again.

She knew – her dream of a fortune had gone. The taste of bile was strong in her throat, but after her peculiar turn she was grateful that was all. No matter, she had other fish to fry. Some things were more important than money.

So it surprised her when Stoehlheim gestured to her with a raised palm, saying: "Miss O'Reilly, the dice are nearest to you – you might as well take your turn."

So she was still in the game – it was now a sideshow, but what the hell?

*

Before Sandra threw again, Stoehlheim had a point to make: "It has possibly escaped you all that more than one of you is just one truthful answer away from being rich..." He paused for effect, "...beyond your wildest dreams." He waited while the players looked at the board. "Then again, I'm sure most of you are more than capable of some wild dreams, so perhaps 'rich commensurate with them' would be a more appropriate phrase. Let me just remind you all that a double six is required to finish."

Having all re-engaged, there was a collective catching of the breath at this reminder.

Sandra ignored what might have been a jibe at her and threw – eight. Next was Emma. The dice rattled in the cup as her hands shook.

Emma's nervous, lame throw brought her a seven. Her relief was evident. Then Andrew threw. Another double six stared back at them, taunting each player according to his or her desserts. "Devil's luck," he said, almost derisively. He took a deep breath and then a *Home Truths* card.

He stared at it, then laughed, an edgy sound, mirthless.

Brad snatched the card from his grasp, read it and then gave a snort of disgust, while pointing at both Sandra and Andrew. "They were right: this is fixed! There's no way that could be the next card."

"What does it say?" asked several voices.

"What would you do if you won a huge fortune?" He flicked the card towards the centre of the table in disgust. "Yes or no answers – my arse!"

"Perhaps it's just in the wrong pile," ventured Emma, but Brad leaned forward and pointed to the words printed on the back – *Home Truths* – which elicited a look from Emma suggesting she would just shut up and retreat to the stupid corner.

"We've wasted our time here. That's all the old fucker Du Fuss wanted – to waste our time and take the piss. Let him rot in hell!"

There were some angry words of agreement. Though no-one dared to accuse or confront Stoehlheim, they all looked in his direction, half-voicing their confusion, but also, deep down, wondering what retribution Brad's outburst would bring.

Then they saw the look on their host's face – he was simply staring at something and smiling. There was an exclamation from Sandra O'Reilly and they all turned towards Andrew.

What they saw confused and shocked them. Andrew Hansen was sitting with his eyes shut, the Bible glowing green beneath his hand. In the sudden silence his token made its final move forward unaided and the exquisite tooled door of the golden cage popped open without a sound.

Not for the first time that night, there was a communal gasp.

Stoehlheim's resonant voice proclaimed: "I believe we have a winner."

As if this were a signal from a hypnotist, Andrew's eyes opened and he looked around him.

Emma asked everyone and no-one: "What did he say?"

There were whispers; conjecture as to the answer he had given, but though Andrew opened his mouth, his voice appeared to have deserted him.

Stoehlheim interjected, "Since none of you saw fit to listen, it is of no consequence to you what he said." The voices of the others rose in renewed protest, Brad's being the most vehement: "Just who the fuck do you think you are? We're the chosen players – we've a right to know!"

Once again the lawyer stood, thick shadows surrounding him as if he were emerging from pitch. He raised his hand. "Be silent." Those who had been contemplating uttering some agreement with Brad found their words rendered almost solid and pushed back into their throats. Now, at the very end, they saw the glint of ice and anger in Stoehlheim's eyes. Too late, they realised that he commanded the space around them. Despite his steel-grey hair and his pallor, he gave an impression of dark strength. The spotlights were unable to dispel the perceptible aura of gloom which seemed to have settled around him. Just his eyes glowed, full of menace.

He turned his aquiline, noble but hard features towards each of them in turn, reserving a lingering look for Brad who looked down and seemed to be having trouble clearing his throat. When he looked at Yvonne, she tried hard to suppress a shudder. The thin, cognisant smile she received from Stoehlheim suggested that she had failed.

*

The room was now so quiet, you could have heard a worm burrowing. They waited.

*

"I wish I could say," said Stoehlheim, contempt dripping from his every syllable, "that I have never witnessed such greed. Unfortunately as a lawyer of many, many years practice, I have seen too much of it." He left his place and moved past their tense figures, circling the table. Each of them looked down as he went by, awaiting some sort of retribution. He stopped behind Brad, who pulled again at the collar of his shirt and slumped slightly when his nemesis moved on. As he passed Emma, she folded her arms across her chest as if cold. It seemed that her breath issued as vapour. As Stoehlheim paced slowly, the leather of his shoes creaked; the boards of an old ship after years on the high seas.

He started a second circuit, but this time stopped at the door. "Mr Hansen, as the winner of the game, I would ask that you remain behind to complete the formalities, sign the necessary documentation and so on." He opened the door as if it had never been locked. "The rest of you, remembering of course that you have signed a non-disclosure agreement, may leave...and may some of you, at least, sleep easily with your consciences – and of course your mobile phones – tonight."

He could read their thoughts – so that was it? As he gestured towards the open door, they looked stunned, dismissed, powerless, robbed even of a period of mourning. They filed out abruptly, leaving behind the faint odour of the detritus of their lives. The lawyer nodded to each of them in turn as they passed. No-one spoke, not even to exchange a word with Andrew Hansen. However...

*

For several minutes, Andrew felt as if he had been struggling towards the surface of a dream. Now he felt a hand squeezing his shoulder. He looked up to find Yvonne Elmer, who smiled at him and then left. Then a much larger hand extended towards him as if offering to pull him clear of that night's shipwreck. He stood and took the proffered hand, which clasped his in a hot, firm grip and shook it.

"Congratulations, Mr Hansen. Please accompany me to my office where I will take the greatest of pleasure in making you a very rich young man."

"I can't help feeling I'll be signing away my soul."

"No, someone took care of that."

He gestured for Andrew to go ahead of him. "I am sure Mr Du Fuss would have approved. May I offer you a celebratory sherry?"

*

They left the room. The Chancery board glinted in the spotlights. Once more there was the faintest hiss of static.

Perhaps in the wake of the heavy boardroom door closing, the door of the cage on the board swung shut.

*

Stoehlheim led the way to his office, opened the door and motioned for Andrew to go in. He gestured towards a chair. The chill from the air-conditioning had struck Andrew straight away and he pulled his jacket a little closer to him when his host wasn't looking.

"May I interest you in that sherry, Mr Hansen?"

"Thank you, but I'm driving."

Andrew watched as Stoehlheim ignored him and continued to pour two sherries from a decanter, one of which he brought over and handed to his guest, who took the proffered drink without protest.

"A wiser move than you know, Mr Hansen. The man who refuses Jerez de Añada a second time may be considered

119

unworthy of good fortune." He paused. "Besides, you can certainly afford a taxi." Smiling, Stoehlheim raised his glass. "To Arthur Du Fuss."

Likewise Andrew raised his glass and responded: "To Arthur Du Fuss."

Stoehlheim headed to a painting behind his desk and Andrew had to comment: "I recognise that too. Isn't it *Faust and Mephistopheles* by Delacroix?"

As before that evening, Stoehlheim nodded his approval. "Quite the aficionado." Now the lawyer pointed to the Munch painting. "No such kudos for knowing that one." He laughed. "But setting that aside, Mr Du Fuss said there was more to you than just an IT geek."

That spooked Andrew a little. "He knew what I did for a living?"

"As one or two people have discovered tonight, he knew much that they wished he didn't. Then again, does that not reflect rather shamefully on them, when you consider that no-one knew what he did?"

While Andrew digested the implicit contradictions of that rhetorical question, Stoehlheim removed the painting from the wall to reveal a safe. He gave Andrew a knowing look. "My other safe." He reached inside and withdrew a sealed envelope. Returning to sit at his desk, he handed it to Andrew. "Perhaps his foresight explains this." Andrew looked at the envelope. "Go ahead." Stoehlheim gestured.

*

It was perhaps strange to see any life in Merryking Close at that late, late hour, but if anyone who understood the shadows of the human soul had been asked to predict which houses might still have found it hard to douse the lights, they would have made accurate guesses.

The downstairs rooms of the Thomas household were in darkness, but two lights were on upstairs. Now one went out.

*

Emma Thomas sat in bed, flicking through a magazine. Darren spoke to her from the en suite bathroom, doing his best to feign indifference.

"You were quiet on the way back tonight." He flicked off the bathroom light and as he entered the bedroom he could tell her thoughts were anywhere but on the printed pages, though she was trying hard to make them her focus. Darren was wearing only his shorts. He remembered a time when the sight of his trim, muscular body would have seen Emma throw aside any other distraction. He rooted through a drawer. "Why was that then?"

"Was what?" She didn't even look up.

"Why were you so quiet? "

"Was I? Well, it was disturbing – the evening. The whole thing."

"You certainly seemed disturbed." He continued to root around in the drawer.

"I'm trying to push it from my mind."

"Why? I thought it was all rather interesting. Amazing what you learn."

"I thought it was creepy." On she flicked through the pages, still refusing to look up from her magazine.

"Is that why you were so worked up?"

"Was I?"

"Yes!" He pulled a T-shirt from the drawer and slammed it shut.

Emma jumped and, at last, gave him her attention. He enjoyed the uncertainty, perhaps even fear, in her eyes, though she tried to sound reproachful. "You scared me."

"You don't know what scared means." He didn't know quite where that came from or was heading, but again relished her good old-fashioned panic. They stared at each other – he won for the second time that night as she looked away. "Then again, you did look like you were shitting yourself at one point tonight..." He waited. "...more than one point."

"It was just a strange atmosphere – threatening. And then Mr Du Fuss's voice, as if he was speaking from the other side. And those counters moving... and don't get me started on the questions."

"And all those secrets."

He had her where he wanted her. The thing escaping him at that precise moment was whether he wanted her there at all.

Emma placed her magazine on the bedside table. "Look, I don't want to talk about it, okay."

She turned on her side, switched off her bedside light and pulled up the covers.

Darren dropped the T-shirt on the floor. He got into the

bed and looked at her with her back turned towards him, the tattoo of his name hidden by the silk dressing gown she had chosen to wear to bed. She'd had it done in a specific spot, just between her shoulder blades, as she said it was a place that – what were her words? – *always got her going*. He found himself wondering whether Brad Llewellyn was privy to that information now.

He moved in closer behind her and placed his hand on her neck. As he sensed the way she tensed, he didn't really know what he had been hoping for. He pushed her hair back from her neck, kissed her and then started to pull down the dressing gown. Without even knowing how, he knew she had opened her eyes and was probably staring straight ahead. He felt her discomfort and her words bore out his suspicions: "If you don't mind, Darren, I'm not in the mood."

"First time for everything." He continued to kiss her neck.

"Darren..." He wasn't in the mood to listen. "Darren, stop." Now he twined his fingers in her hair and pulled. "Ow! You're hurting me."

"Thought that was foreplay for you."

He released her hair, pushing her head down into the pillow as he did so before turning away and flopping down on his back.

*

Emma stared into the void, biting her lip.

*

Darren's eyes, too, stared at and through the ceiling. They were unreadable.

*

The other house showing a light, like a Cornish wrecker luring a ship onto the rocks, was Sandra O'Reilly's.

She stood in her bathrobe, staring into the bathroom mirror. Now she picked up a rectangle of card from the edge of the washbasin, lifted it, examined it. It was one of the *Home Truths* cards. She read out loud: "Have you ever taken something from someone, knowing it would hurt them deeply?"

Sandra looked over her shoulder in the general direction of the Close, with hatred in her eyes. She looked back at the mirror and then screamed "Fuck off!" as she smashed her palm against the glass, cracking it.

It was some time before she broke away from staring at her own distorted reflection and started to dress her wounds.

CHAPTER 8

On autopilot, Yvonne slammed her front door, but then winced as the sound echoed around the Close. She put down the smart overnight case, locked the door and then set off.

On any other day she would have been buzzing at the prospect of the day ahead – a trip into the City, a very wealthy client up for grabs and a stopover in one of London's deluxe hotels on the South Bank with an amazing view across towards St Paul's in one direction and Tower Bridge in the other. Being on the South Bank always gave her a thrill, with its vibrancy and hints of a darker past. But after the events of the previous night, darkness had taken on a new meaning. It had left her with a hangover of conscience, the like of which even her more morally ambiguous legal victories had failed to inflict – hence her cringing at the noise of the front door banging shut.

Looking across the Close, she saw Brad Llewellyn standing in his bathrobe gazing out of the window, phone pressed to one ear. They exchanged half smiles.

As she walked on, her heels seemed to resound through the enclosed street. She was moving at a slightly slower pace than usual, looking at each house in turn, trying to piece together what the game of Chancery had meant for each of them. The curtains were still drawn in Andrew Hansen's house. No conjecture required there. "Guess you don't need to head off to work anymore," she said under her breath.

On cue, on the other side of the street she saw Celia Braddock's curtains twitch as she peeped out from behind the nets. Yvonne gave a dismissive shake of her head towards the crone.

Despite her already hesitant pace, her steps faltered as she passed Arthur's house and her eyes were drawn to the upstairs windows. She looked away again and a shudder passed through her – but as she did so, her gaze fell on Sandra O'Reilly's downstairs windows. There was no-one there.

Last to fall under her scrutiny was the home of Emma and Darren Thomas. Her thoughts were troubled as she remembered her conversation with Emma about her marital issues. The body language between the two of them – husband and wife – last night and the implications of one or two responses hadn't made for good listening or observation, even without prior knowledge.

She continued to her car, though it was the strangest feeling when she felt compelled to turn again and take in the Close, almost as if some sixth sense were telling her the place would be different on her return. She had to force herself to get into the car and drive away.

*

As the winter sun passed in serenity across Merryking Close that day, where the most dramatic event was a rain squall that lasted a couple of minutes, it was hard to imagine that a cancer was festering in each home. There was a glorious sunset, a stunning interplay of light and shade. Only someone with second sight would have appreciated the wonderful irony of the windows glowing gold on one side of the street while darkness reigned on the other.

*

Darren Thomas stepped out into the cold darkness. The late shift beckoned. He turned and patted Biggles: "Be good, fella." His next words were directed towards the stairs.

"See you tomorrow evening then."

"Okay – bye!" Emma's response from off-screen caused him to look with wistful regret towards the first floor. Then Darren headed off towards his car and his night shift.

He didn't get far. Hit by a sudden resolve, after a couple of hundred yards he turned down a side-street, parked up and killed the engine, before sitting, lost in thought.

Unaware of his presence, a young couple walked past. They stopped a few yards away, giggling, and then kissed passionately, fondling each other with great intimacy before walking on.

Darren smashed the heel of his palm against the steering wheel.

"Fuck the night shift! Fuck everything!"

He got out of the car. As he headed back towards the Close, it dawned on him that he had kissed Emma goodbye for the last time when he had departed for a night shift he would now never make.

He couldn't close his eyes to it any more, now that her infidelity had been spray-canned on the wall for him and, perhaps most heartbreaking of all, for others to see. He turned off, treading with stealth down an alleyway that ran behind the houses, skirting the back gardens of Numbers Two, Four, and Six until he emerged at the far end of the Close and hid in some bushes by the last house, that of Brad Llewellyn.

As he stood there, waiting for the curtain to rise, Darren could acknowledge now that he had only ever been in lust with his wife. From their earliest teenage fumbling in his car he had been obsessed with her body. She had grown more desirable with the years. Her billowing curves were the main reason why he always came too quickly and he lived with the fear that other men would satisfy her where he could not. This, combined with his Celtic melancholy, had precipitated the occasional, shaming blows he had dealt her. It didn't help that his career was stagnant. More than once he had cursed the inverse snobbery of the tiny community in which he had grown up, where no-one sought to rise above their station, even less so looked to leave their village, but rather gloried in their humility; extolling in beer-laden rapture the joys of spending your life on your knees hacking at a coal face. Emma, on the other hand, had gone to night school and was now the manager of the air import department in a thriving freight forwarding company, where stock options had enabled her to fund the house in this exclusive little road. Darren still earned good money, mainly because of the overtime that he was prepared to work at the warehouse. Now he realised that he had been away too many nights.

It was sometimes his fervent wish that he could break adrift from Emma. Some nights, fuelled by alcohol and a bonding session with his friends, he would feel that he could live without her. But then he would see her in her lingerie applying make-up, or with some silky blouse or tight skirt caressing her wanton figure, and he would recognise that his physical desire for his wife overrode every other single reason he had for being. Nor could he bear the thought of any other man enjoying her, and if he left her, that's what would happen. Another man's penis would enter her, fuck her. She would suck some stranger's cock and swallow his cum. Hands other than his own would squeeze her breasts.

Like they haven't already, ventured the darkness.

Darren had to screw his eyes shut, trying once more to close out the increasingly sordid graphic images with which he constantly tortured himself. They had become unbearable since last night. He was a man on a rack, stretched beyond endurance, each spiteful second host to a lifetime's pain. He welcomed what he would see tonight. If he could edge beyond this Limbo of inactivity, then he could move on.

Some indeterminate length of time later, probably only minutes, he heard a door open and the click of it being shut with great care. There was the clip-clop of heels. Darren glanced out to see his wife taking her quick little steps, though to his surprise she headed out left onto the main street. Biggles wasn't in tow, so this was not a dog walk. That in itself made Darren's heart sink; she loved the dog, so whatever reason she had for being out, it was something that made her break the rules.

As the sound of her heels disappeared, he emerged from his hiding place, crossing at speed to another position behind the garage block, from which he could see Brad Llewellyn's back garden. He expected to hear her approaching steps and was thrilled, though that was laced with a perverse disappointment, to hear nothing. He risked a quick glance out, but withdrew his head swiftly into the shadows as he saw his wife's familiar curves approaching on bare feet, her shoes in her hand.

Hearing the latch of the garden gate opening, he risked another look. Emma hurried up the path towards the back door of the house, which creaked open as if by magic upon her approach. Light fell on her and she disappeared inside without saying a word.

It was not an upstairs light being switched off or the drawing of the curtains that pushed Darren Thomas over the edge; rather it was the shocking intimacy of his wife's stockinged feet as she skipped along the back alleyway and up the garden path.

Darren leaned back against a wall, face contorted with despair. He whispered: "The night shift."

*

She had already screamed and shuddered her way to two apparently very intense orgasms, but there was no stopping her tonight. He had never known her as wild as this, from the moment she had stepped through the front door and he had turned from closing it to find her hands grasping at his trouser belt. Now, on the bed to which he had almost had to drag her, she leaned back and ground her groin against him as another moaning storm gathered intensity. She moved in an increasing frenzy, gasping, drenched in sweat. He could feel the onset of his own orgasm and reached up to grab those beautiful breasts. She looked at him with depravation in her eyes, her words wild: "That's right, squeeze them! Hurt me! Fuck me!"

It was too much for a hot-blooded man, but he managed to hold on long enough for her to come again, screaming, before he spent himself. Now she flopped, sweating beside him and they recovered their breath.

At length he whistled. "Jeez, Emma, I've never known you be like that!" She reached up, touched his face and laughed, then moved her hand down and cupped him. A lazy, but salacious sigh followed. They stared up at the ceiling. Then Emma rolled over and propped herself on her elbows, a sight that never failed to stir him as it accentuated the curve of her buttocks and her deep cleavage.

"You know," she said, "it might well be because I was so convinced yesterday that I was going to lose this." She moved her hand once again and squeezed his balls. "But we escaped. Maybe it's a reaction to that. How the hell did you do it Brad? How did we get away with it?'

He reached over to his nightstand for a cigarette. There was something smug in the studied insouciance of the action, though as he blew out the first lungful of smoke, his breath quivered. Then he propped himself up on one elbow and said: "I've read about people who say that they can pass a lie detector test, cheat the machine. Most of them did it by creating their own reality, telling themselves that something is true often enough that to their minds and instincts it ceases to be a lie."

He took another deep drag and exhaled while he paused to reflect. The memory of those edgy, electric moments by the Chancery table had a sudden vividness, as if he had closed a door on them in the intervening hours, but they had simply lurked, waiting. Now they wandered back into the light. With them came the taunting reminder that he had missed out on the money – but hanging back in the shadows was the very real presence of Stoehlheim. Somehow, Brad knew the money was a paradox; losing out on it had been an escape of sorts. Now he found himself running his fingers along his throat.

He drew deeply again on the cigarette and continued: "The reason I took so long to answer the question yesterday was that I was trying to focus on the positives, the half-truths. You see, since I'm not married, in one way I could claim that I had never had an affair. Okay, it was a gamble, a technicality, but under the circumstances, what the hell? It worked."

Now Emma's lips were on his again. She sucked hungrily at the bottom lip, then gave him a wink, a knowing look and said: "Such a clever boy." Her lips moved down his chest. "Clever boy deserves a present." She pushed him onto his back.

"Do you think he knows?"

His words provoked only the briefest of pauses in the inexorable journey her mouth was making and her words were punctuated by nips and kisses. "No, I don't think he has a clue, and quite frankly, at this moment I don't care."

He was hard again and Emma plunged him into her mouth. *Quite frankly*, thought Brad, *at this moment neither do I.*

*

Sandra O'Reilly paced up and down her living room, still in her work clothes, her arms folded in a protective barrier across her midriff. In one hand she held her third large whisky of the evening, in the other her umpteenth cigarette.

She paused each time she passed the cabinet containing the Cinderella scene, staring at the space where the coach should have stood.

She hated being like this. For someone successful and apparently desirable to both sexes, how pathetic it was to feel empty and used up in this way. But that was what happened when something you craved had been taken from you.

Placing the smouldering cigarette amongst the bones of many others in the ashtray, she picked up the card lying next to it – the *Home Truths* card she had pocketed at the

Chancery table – and read aloud, as she had so many times since that fateful evening: "Have you ever taken something from someone, knowing it would hurt them deeply?"

She took yet another long drag on the cigarette, almost as if she hoped it would choke her. This was all because of the poisonous jealousy and malice of an old woman, one who existed only through the lives of others, like a parasite. Frustrated old hag.

Though Sandra was loath to admit it, that wrinkled bitch was another reason why she didn't bring men back to her house. Word got about, or at least Celia Braddock, for whom knowledge was power, ensured that it did. Sandra had some standing in the community through her business. She did not intend to lose that through her appetites. One near miss with Brad had been enough.

With each circuit of her living room, she felt her anger mounting as she looked at the showcase. The missing glass coach had been a limited edition so there was little chance of finding one for sale. Cinderella, the prince and the wicked stepmother were all there. Sandra shook her head as she sought to marginalise her despair.

"For God's sake – you're forty-one!"

Yet at forty-one, despite having more than she had ever dared to hope for, she was still the little girl in the empty bedroom whose mother had to work on Christmas Day. As she looked into the mahogany showcase, she saw only the space where the fairy tale was incomplete. Once, Sandra had been at work when she received an email telling her a parcel had been delivered, left in her designated safe place behind a large plant – not ideal, but she didn't trust her neighbours, or at least the one she knew was usually home – but it had not been there when she returned.

Now things were falling into place. She remembered, on another occasion, hearing the familiar desiccated voice of Celia Braddock, who must have been making her way down the Close towards the main road. It had caused Sandra to hang back indoors, not wanting to go out and cross paths, or swords, with the crone. She was talking to the postman: "Another toy for the little girl at Number One?" She didn't catch the postman's response. Of course the boxes were distinctive, most with the name of the porcelain manufacturer written on them, so they were clearly a tempting target, but not until yesterday during the game of Chancery had Sandra known without doubt that Celia Braddock had taken any of her things.

She drained her whisky glass in one shot and poured another.

*

Back in the now illusory comfortable familiarity of his home, Darren was up in the loft, pushing aside cardboard boxes. He wiped cobwebs from his hands and coughed as dust entered his throat.

"Where are you?" More muttering and shoving aside of boxes. "I know I put you...ah!"

He lifted a small, battered wooden case, which he held closer to the light while he released the catches. Opening it, he placed it down with respect and withdrew a long, shining bayonet. In awe, he looked at the gleaming blade.

Then his features crumpled with despair. He wiped his sleeve across his eyes, gathering himself together before climbing down from the loft, weapon in hand.

*

Inside Number One, Merryking Close, Sandra was still pacing, smoking, drinking. Stopping for the umpteenth time in the middle of the room, she squeezed her eyes shut, opened them again, staring at the same cabinet, but also through it and the wall beyond. Draining yet another glass of whisky, she put it down on the table with a bang. Even though she had all the proof she needed in Celia Braddock's *Home Truths* card, she could not believe that she had been giving serious consideration to going over and confronting the old witch.

She was still in this state of disbelief as the cold night air pressed through her blouse while she stood outside Celia's door.

*

Andrew Hansen sat staring at the TV. There was football on, but it could as easily have been a programme about knitting, so little was he taking in. It was, however, proving companionable as background noise – and as a taste of reality after the otherworldly events of the night before.

He hadn't appreciated just how on edge he was until the burst from the doorbell made him jump. Though his feet felt leaden and his mind distracted as he made his way to the door, once he opened it to find nobody there, his senses were knife-edge keen. He was spooked, that was beyond doubt.

Stepping outside with caution, he looked to the right. A noise to his left.

He spun back, just as a figure stepped towards him – and smiled in relief as the pizza delivery man addressed him: "Sorry, sir, the receipt blew away. This isn't a street where you want to leave litter!"

"No problem." His racing pulse gave that response the lie – and again it was a measure of his distraction that he had forgotten all about ordering the pizza.

"So that's a large pepperoni and a large hot 'n' spicy, sir. You extra hungry, or just feeling lucky?" The delivery man laughed.

"Both – thank you." He handed the man a five-pound note. "That's for you."

The delivery man looked at it amazed. "Thank you very much, sir! You have a great evening."

The footsteps faded and Andrew headed for the door. However, just before stepping inside, something caused him to hesitate. He looked up and down the Close, cocked his head and listened, unsure exactly what he had been expecting. With a shrug, he headed in.

CHAPTER 9

In response to the insistent ringing of another doorbell, Celia Braddock exited her lounge, shuffling and muttering. Perhaps the strangest part was that she was even bothering. It wasn't her custom to open the front door after dark and as she headed down the hallway along a threadbare Indian runner rug, she had to wonder whether the events of the previous night had disorientated here, or had it simply been the memories, dredged from the mud to which she had once consigned an innocent dog? Was the truth of it that, deep down, tonight she did not want to be alone? Maybe, just for once, she welcomed human interaction, rather than communing with angry spirits, even if it were an untrustworthy lad selling sponges, or some lying political party candidate.

It wouldn't have been right, though, if Celia didn't feel anger at the persistence of whoever was disturbing her. The distorted chiming was shredding her nerves.

Once at the door, she stood on tiptoes and squinted through the frosted fanlight. Unable to identify the visitor, she put on the chain and opened the door a crack.

Again, in some ways it was a surprising comfort to see

Sandra O'Reilly standing there, but the look on that woman's face told Celia that the relief would be short-lived.

There was something disturbing about her appearance, still in her work blouse and skirt, but looking slightly dishevelled and flushed. Already, Celia could smell how much she had been smoking. Sandra stood there with her arms folded across her chest. She looked in the mood for a confrontation. Still Celia was taken aback by the vehemence of her tone.

"You took it didn't you?" Sandra swayed a little.

So she was drunk then – nothing new there.

"I beg your pardon. What are you talking about?"

Celia made to close the door, but stopped, curious as Sandra revealed a piece of card she'd been holding, which she started to read, mimicking Celia's voice: "Have you ever taken something from someone, knowing it would hurt them deeply?"

Now Celia grew nervous, but held her ground. "Have you gone mad?" She went to close the door again, but Sandra put her hand out to stop her.

"You took it, didn't you?" she repeated the accusation.

Rather than closing the door, Celia held it open for some reason. "I beg your pardon – what are you talking about?"

"Cinderella's coach. You stole it from me, you old witch!" Celia remained silent. "Cinderella's coach," repeated Sandra, both angry and in a state of drunken distraction. "It was a limited edition and you stole it from me."

Now Celia's eyes narrowed with comprehension. "Ah, you're talking about one of your little trinkets. Well, let me tell you, I wouldn't steal yours because I have my own. In this instance, I can understand why you are a bit over-wrought. It is a beautiful thing. Normally I don't bother with such things, but that one I had to have."

"What?" Sandra was stunned.

"Yes. Franklin Mint. You're right, it was a limited edition, advertised on the back of the Telegraph. I too have a small, but selective collection, and it was such a precious piece..."

"What!? Liar! I heard you talking to the postman one morning before I had left the house." Again she impersonated Celia. "Another toy for the little girl at Number One."

"Hmm, so that's proof of theft these days, is it?"

That stopped Sandra in her tracks for a moment.

Celia was strangely unprepared for her visitor's next move. The latter narrowed her eyes and put her shoulder to the door with surprising strength, splintering the wood holding the chain. Celia staggered backwards as Sandra strode into the hallway. "Where is it?"

"Get out of my house!" Celia was genuinely fearful now as Sandra O'Reilly shoved her out of the way and made for the lounge. "You can't do this! I'll call the police."

"Not if I call them first," was Sandra's retort as she stormed into the living room.

"I..I..I..have the receipt," said the old woman frantically as she tailed the intruder.

Once Sandra had disappeared into the lounge, Celia headed for the stairs.

*

Sandra scanned the living room. It smelled of what she liked to term 'old fogey's musk', a curious mixture of talcum powder, soap and some underlying, less pleasant odour. Her eyes took in the dated dresser, coffee table, chintzy furniture. She stomped over to a Victorian writing bureau, sending papers flying as she wrenched it open. Finding no ornaments, she climbed onto a chair to inspect the top shelf of the dresser, where there were indeed a couple of collectibles; nothing like the number she possessed and certainly not of the same quality, although, in a moment of peculiar detachment, she recognised a couple of Danbury Mint pieces.

Having failed to find what she was looking for, she slammed the door shut and crossed to the window. She pulled the curtains back with such force, a vase of tulips toppled over and smashed.

Then she became aware of the silence. The old bitch had not followed her into the room and Sandra figured that what she now heard was the creaking of a staircase. She rushed back into the hallway in time to see Celia making her way with arthritic slowness up the stairs.

Younger and fitter, she took the stairs two at a time, pushed past Celia and went into what looked like the main bedroom. As she did so she gagged slightly, while she took in furniture and fittings of a similar age and ilk to those downstairs and said: "Whatever scent you're applying, it's not enough to cover the stench of urine..."

She tailed off, eyes widening as she saw, on top of an old marble mantelpiece, the holy grail – a solid glass pumpkin with a gold-plated frame and wheels.

Sandra crossed to the fireplace, picked up the coach, almost with reverence, and felt its satisfying heaviness. She turned now to find Celia Braddock scowling in the doorway. "That's my property. I have the receipt. Put it back."

"Liar! We both know who this belongs to."

"I shall call the police."

"Do your worst."

Sandra headed for the door. The old woman would not stand aside. "So you're a thief as well as a whore." Sandra's eyes narrowed. The words still had the power to shock her, though not as much as what followed as Celia continued: "Just like your mother where the latter is concerned."

With her mouth gaping, Sandra would not have been able to articulate a response, even if she could have thought of something suitable. But there was nothing and Celia drove the blade home.

"Oh, we all knew what she was doing on her..." She paused for emphasis, "...night-shifts."

"What do you know about...?"

"Be sure, I knew Eunice O'Reilly – probably one of the few people who didn't know her in the biblical sense. The apple didn't fall very far from the tree, did it? No amount of expensive toys will change that."

Now Sandra felt something which had lain long dormant at the bottom of the black lake start to rise. It took the form of a female face, not seen for many years, and it remained slightly distorted just below the surface of the water. It was a woman who had been forced to work at night as well as in the day to help her family survive. Her breath had often smelled of alcohol as she came to tuck Sandra into bed. Sometimes there had been other smells, almost, but not quite, masked by the drink, but these had gone by the morning. That woman had needed love and all the hope that it can bring, but as it passed her by, so she gave it instead, in the only way she knew. Only when they had taken all the love she had to give had home had become a violent place.

Despite herself, Sandra bent forward and retched in a sudden, violent spasm. She looked up at Celia between gagging fits and said: "How dare you!" Lifting one hand, she slapped Celia across the face. Shocked, Celia clasped her cheek, while Sandra pushed on: "It's too sad. YOU are sad, living your miserable, lonely life." She turned, looked at the bedroom and shook her head. "If you can call it a life, through the actions of others – and to compensate for that, you spit poison at them." Sandra straightened up. "If you feel by taking something of mine you can somehow be me, you're wrong. Spying through your window because you're too fucking scared to turn and look at the emptiness of your own world."

Celia's mouth opened. Her eyes were blazing. Now she drew herself up to her full height and Sandra was taken aback by how tall the crone was without her stoop. Some colour had fought its way into her normally ashen skin. "Monstrous!"

"You're the monster. You've earned that name trying to suck the life out of anyone who stumbles into your lair."

"Get out of my house!"

"Not without this." Sandra brandished the glass coach in front of Celia's face.

"As I said, a thief and a little whore."

The former insult goaded Sandra more than the latter now. She stepped right up into Celia's face. "I think we both know who the thief is around here."

"A drunken sot as well, judging by your breath."

"Judging by yours, I'd say you've been eating shit."

Fuelled by the indignity of those words, Celia Braddock lifted her hand and struck Sandra O'Reilly across the face, a surprisingly powerful blow. It seemed that anger had given the old woman strength and Sandra was forced to back off a couple of paces, holding her face. The coach fell from her grasp, but the solid glass didn't smash. As she held her cheek, she thought again of the childhood she had been in such a desperate hurry to leave – but whatever her faults, her mother had not been like this.

She turned on Celia, her eyes narrowing menacingly: "How dare you!? How dare you do any of this!? I imagine that any woman who ever allowed a man inside her must seem like a whore to you." She gestured towards the old woman's groin. "You would have split like dried timber if your husband had ever forced his way between your legs." She stood eyeball to eyeball with Celia, noticing the crust where spittle had gathered at the corners of the old woman's mouth. "When you lie alone at night, do you hear the groans of pleasure from the houses around you? Do they fill you with fear? I can't imagine that you were ever wet enough to enjoy sex." Celia's mouth gaped in silent protest, drool bridging her upper and lower dentures. "Ah, I see you're in denial? Maybe you were a wanton slut who liked it in an era when people would not have approved. Maybe that's your problem. Maybe your life has been one long process of self-loathing."

The drool formed a tendril, which started to fall. Sandra watched its accelerating descent and then looked back into the crone's eyes, saying: "You disgust me."

Shoving Celia to one side, Sandra stooped to snatch the coach from the floor and made her way out of the bedroom, only to find herself pulled back by the hair. She gasped and tried to continue on her way towards the top of the stairs, but Celia wasn't giving way and managed to grasp the coach. Sandra was taken aback by the sight, but more so the strength of the sinewy, liver-spotted hands.

"Give...it...up," panted Celia, each word parenthesised by a tug at the *objet d'art*.

"Never!" Sandra clung on, though horrified by the sight of the bulging-eyed, frothing witch who refused to let her escape; this thing of nightmares, a suburban Gagool, Gollum without the possibility of redemption.

And still it was wailing. "Let go, you thieving, drunken slut!"

No, she was Celia Braddock after all, doing what she did best and fate had just put her undoing in Sandra's hands, in the shape of the solid glass pumpkin of the coach, which had worked loose from the gold frame. Sandra drew back her arm, saying: "You want it…" and, to the accompaniment of the words "…take it!", she smashed the orb into the old woman's face with all the rage she had never allowed herself to express in her younger years.

There was a sickening 'THOCK' as the glass met bone and cartilage. Blood spattered. Celia put her hands to her face with a rasping cry of agony. Viscous red fluid seeped between her fingers as she dropped to the floor.

The problem now for Sandra, apart from the fact that she appeared to have killed Celia Braddock, was the position of Celia's hands, pressed as they were to the dying woman's face and therefore no longer taking her killer's weight on the gold frame of the coach. As she staggered backwards, like someone who had pulled too hard on a Christmas cracker, Sandra stepped into the void, plummeting down the stairs, her neck broken and her life gone even before the pumpkin finished its jaunty, bouncing progress to nestle by her side.

As if nature and the night were disgusted by what they had seen, the front door swung shut.

*

Rule One – if you were fucking another man's wife, you needed a decent Chubb lock on the back door of your house.

The black humour in that thought and the slight smile it brought to his lips surprised Darren as he turned the handle and with great caution stepped inside the playboy's kitchen.

He closed the door again with care, but then given the amount of noise that reached his ears now from upstairs, realised he could probably have smashed a window to break in and not have been heard. Besides, it was no louder than a breaking heart.

Now he moved to the foot of the stairs; started the ascent. A groan of especial ecstasy caused his stride to falter for a moment and his hands to take a tighter grip of the banister, but then he moved on.

*

Incredibly he was hard again. The woman certainly knew what to do with her mouth. Then, as she looked up at him and said: "Put me on my knees, Brad, take me from behind," he felt himself going as rigid as a rock. This was turning into the fuck of fucks.

He doffed an imaginary cap to Arthur Du Fuss; Brad may not have won the fortune, but his ticket had certainly come up. Tonight, he was with every man's dream whore. In a moment of distraction, he wondered when he would tire of her. Not imminently, that was for sure. Positioning himself with the help of her eager fingers, he thrust deep, to her evident pleasure.

She looked over her shoulder at him again, her eyes full of sluttishness: "You bad boy! Don't you know I'm married?" Her laugh was dirtiness itself. She knew full well what her words were doing to him: "Yes Brad! Oh fuck yeah!"

*

Cliché though it sounded, Emma had never felt like this – at least nowhere other than in her mind. As more waves pulsed through her stomach, she wanted to scream her ecstasy, celebrate her rebirth, which was the only term she could find to describe the sense of release she had experienced the previous night on her emergence from the lawyer's office. At the time, she had put this down solely to avoiding the revelation of her affair. But as she and Darren had driven home in the peculiar silence, she recalled the look in Stoehlheim's eyes as he had bid her farewell. At the time it had made her shiver, but in the car she realised that what she had seen was something primal and the savagery of it had touched her; excited her.

He was a strange one, the lawyer; old, but radiating strength from his surprisingly powerful body. Now, on her knees, she closed her eyes and allowed herself to imagine him, his tool hard and white as ivory. She was so turned on it seemed that her lover's cock had grown to the very proportions she was imagining.

It was perverse – although Emma had been relieved that her affair had not been discovered, she knew now that she could not stay with Darren. He was a good man most of the time, but she needed more. His jealousy smothered her, drove her to what she was doing now. If she had been physically satisfied in their relationship, perhaps she could have coped with the possessiveness, might even have felt some herself. But Brad Llewellyn had helped her move on a few pages in life's dictionary and right now, as he pounded against her, they were certainly exploring the entries under 'F'.

She felt the pressure building again, the sensitive pulsing, which signalled the onset of yet another orgasm, and closed her eyes in anticipation. But suddenly and all too soon, she felt Brad stiffen and let out a moaning, choking gasp as he spent himself inside her.

Despite her disappointment, she carried on playing her part in this wild play: "Yes Brad! God, I love it when you come!"

She lowered herself onto her stomach and he collapsed on top of her breathing heavily in her ear. He gave a choking, growling groan, shuddered; whispered: "Emma...Emma..." He seemed exhausted and was in a profuse sweat. Well, on reflection, she had been pretty demanding tonight.

That was when she noticed the warm fluid between his stomach and her back, as she tried to shift his weight slightly. At first, she thought that he must have pulled out of her rather quickly, but there seemed to be a lot of fluid, too much for a man who had come inside her not twenty minutes before. She touched her side, frowned and brought the fingertips into view. On seeing the blood, she tried turning her head, but he was so heavy now and, without knowing how, she knew that he was dead, even before his head lolled over her shoulder.

Shuddering, she tried to turn and push his dead weight off her, but found it almost impossible to move.

It was the disembodied voice, familiar yet alien in its coldness, that caused her to lose control of her bladder. She could feel his breath on the back of her neck. "I love you," it said. Those words of endearment had never provoked such horror.

*

When he had entered the room, he had surprised himself by just standing frowning, mouth open, hands by his side. His head had fallen to one side as he watched with intent, almost puzzled. There was a peculiar sense of detachment.

That had changed when he became aware of the sound of Brad thrusting against Emma's buttocks.

Now, he stepped forward and stabbed Brad Llewellyn between the shoulder-blades. The bayonet, which had earned Infantryman Dafydd Thomas honour and glory at Rourke's Drift and had been treasured ever since, added an inglorious episode to its history.

Just as Brad started to fall forward, Darren caught sight of the tattoo of his name on Emma's back. To that point, he hadn't been sure whether he would kill her too. Her lover's body fell across her now, she too fell forward onto the bed and Darren moved to straddle the two of them. His wife sealed her fate with her next words: "Yes Brad! God, I love it when you come!"

Now he wanted her to suffer, to know exactly what was happening and who was wielding the scythe. He leaned forward and whispered in her ear: "I love you," while at the same time putting all his weight on the hilt of the bayonet.

On through into her it went. Emma thrashed like a fish on a spear. She tried to scream, but with a firm yet gentle hand he held her head down into the pillow, stifling her words until they started turning to blood. Her spasms grew weaker and finally she stopped moving.

Darren withdrew the blade, shoved Brad's body to one side and sat on the edge of the bed by Emma stroking her hair. He noticed how the blade had entered her almost on the tattoo.

Leaning forward, he kissed her cheek. It struck him now that what he had taken to be their last kiss, as he had left the house that morning, had not been the final goodbye after all.

He continued to stroke her hair while staring at the wall with unseeing eyes and repeating: "Shush, shush now. It's okay. It's all over."

CHAPTER 10

Andrew Hansen sat chewing on the last piece of bacon, staring out of the window. On waking, for once he had made himself a proper breakfast.

*

He couldn't know what a wise move that was, because there is nothing worse than dry retching.

*

He had hardly eaten the previous day, in fact not properly since before that surreal Monday evening at 'Stoehlheim and Stoehlheim'. The lawyer had been charm and courtesy personified as he had led Andrew through the formalities, which would culminate in a huge fortune being transferred into his bank account as soon as was legally possible. While Stoehlheim had given Andrew no grounds for the discomfort he felt during every minute in his presence, the documentation on the other hand, had thrown him, leaving him feeling that the foundations of his, indeed everybody's, world were nothing but sand.

Though he had gone to work as usual the following day – there was no point in counting your chickens – his mind had not been on the job, going over and over the events of that previous evening, trying to work out exactly what had happened. From time to time he had even looked at himself in a mirror, convinced that he would find he had changed in some way.

At length, he had made an excuse about feeling unwell and left early. On his arrival home, unusually for him, he had poured a large drink before flopping in front of the TV, hoping he might find something that would help him relax. The banalities of daytime TV had barely registered with him – though on reflection, if they had, that might have been a much more worrisome tale! – and the delivery pizzas he'd ordered had remained almost untouched.

As he continued chewing and staring now, he shook his head. He believed, despite the previous day's discomfort, what had truly bothered him was that there had appeared to be no-one at home when he'd attempted to revisit the guilt he felt at winning Arthur's fortune. This had unsettled him and he had finally gone to bed, though he was not tired.

So, it was yet another in the long list of surprises when he awoke refreshed after a long, dreamless sleep.

At last, he smiled. He would just bum another day off sick. Who cared what management thought? Andrew was unwilling to spend this gloriously sunny morning at home.

He jumped up, pulled on his jacket and patted the breast pocket to find his wallet. Having checked his Costa card was in there, he grabbed his laptop, before staring at it and putting it down again.

"Old habits die hard."

With a smile, he headed for the door.

On leaving the house, the smile faded. The sense of something being amiss was immediate and tangible, though there was nothing obvious. The Close had a peculiar, deserted feel to it, the weird part being on your average workday morning it was indeed mostly uninhabited. Glancing towards Number Four, he knew that allowed for the emptiness of Celia Braddock's soul and conscience.

What about Arthur? He was always home.

The voice of his own conscience spoke up, reminding him he wasn't exactly welcome on the moral high ground himself. He tried to shake off the guilt and return to his previous observations, looking again at Celia's downstairs window. Most mornings her curtains would be twitching, but today – nothing. Glancing around, he took in the other houses. It was hard to describe, but it was as if the strands and aura of everyday activity were absent from the air. He shrugged. Perhaps it was paranoia. Maybe he feared that everyone was avoiding him now that he had beaten them to a fortune which most of them had so palpably wanted more than he.

But no, thinking about it, he couldn't recall hearing anyone's movements that morning. True, he had slept deeply, but he had been awake at a reasonable hour.

Perhaps it was the need to break the eerie stillness that caused him to start singing under his breath as he set off down the Close.

"We're in the money; we're in the money..."

He stopped, realising he was standing in front of Arthur's house. Andrew's smile faded.

"I'm sorry...really, I am." He continued to address the house, "Is this what it does to us?"

He looked once more in the direction of Celia Braddock's place, as if a sign of life from there might guide his lost ship; a coast to be avoided, but which showed you were still afloat and heading the right way. Still there was nothing; no hint of movement. Unusual indeed.

Feeling a sudden chill in the still, cool air of the shady Close, he zipped up his jacket. He set off once more, but couldn't help turn again. Total silence...

...and then a dog howled.

Andrew shivered, pulled his jacket closer still and walked on, looking at each house in turn. As he walked past Emma and Darren Thomas' place there was more howling and he spotted the lace curtains pushed to one side, held open by the head of Biggles as he looked out. The little, jowled face always brought a smile to Andrew's.

But now Biggles started howling again. This was unusual. Occasionally he barked at passing things, people, cats, leaves, the usual dog stuff. Andrew waited, hoping that the lovely mistress might be at home and come to the window, but the clamour continued and started to make the hairs stand up on the back of his neck. It was unusual for Biggles to be left on his own during the week. If Emma and Darren were both working day shifts he was taken to stay with Emma's mother.

There was no mistaking the fear that resonated.

Okay, thought Andrew, *I'm jumpy enough*, and indeed, his instincts were feeling a bit wired. He moved towards the Thomas' front door, the baying growing louder and more agitated the closer he came.

Andrew spoke in Biggles's direction, though he suspected his words were emollient for his own nerves: "Wassup fella – mum and dad left you home alone?"

He rang the bell. It sounded as if Biggles was on his hind legs, scratching now at the door with his forepaws in obvious distress. Andrew waited long enough for someone to have left the toilet or recovered their composure after any sexual activity, then rang the bell again. The barking grew more frantic.

At last, he crouched down, opened the letterbox and peered through. Reeling back, he put his hands on his knees and breathed deeply. He felt the blood draining from his head. The barking had become frenzied. He stood, unsteady on his atrophied legs. "Okay boy." The words were addressed to Biggles but might just as easily have been meant to self-calm. He forced himself to look through the letterbox again. "Okay boy."

Andrew found his mobile – had to call the police – but then pocketed the phone again while Biggles provided incidental, nerve-tearing music. On reflection, if there was the remotest chance that the person inside – Darren Thomas, he assumed – was alive, he had to get to him now.

The front door was wooden, which made him less hesitant about putting his shoulder to it than if it had been glass.

He knew he might be wasting his time if it was deadbolted – almost laughed in hysteria at the terrible aptness of that term – but thankfully it wasn't and at the sixth impact the lock gave, leaving Andrew to fall through into the hallway.

Biggles stopped barking and cowered on the floor, whimpering. Andrew looked up.

Now that he could see more than dangling feet, it was obvious that Darren Thomas was beyond help. It was a livid sight, one that guaranteed the return of Andrew's breakfast.

Having recovered his composure enough to find a lead and secure Biggles, who pressed in gratitude and fear against his rescuer's legs, Andrew now called the police.

*

He couldn't know it was not to be the worst or strangest sight of that morning.

*

While some officers demarcated the scene of the incident, others attempted to conduct house-to-house enquiries. One glance through another letterbox, that of the immediate neighbouring property, was enough to convince them that they would have to force an entry there too and the door opened onto the second gruesome discovery.

Andrew, still clutching Biggles on a lead and no longer sure who was providing greater comfort to whom, was trying the best he could to answer the questions of the man he assumed was the detective in charge of the case, while at the same time still absorbing further dreadful news. It seemed the back door to Number Six had been found open and some officers had entered. If the finds in Numbers Two and Four weren't already enough to arouse their suspicions, the trail of muddy footprints leading in from the door to the foot of the stairs suggested a further way-marker along the road to Hell. They had found a horrific scene in one of the upstairs bedrooms. Andrew hadn't needed to be Sherlock to work out what it might comprise and why Darren had chosen to go on his own terms.

Now calls from the officers at Number Four drew everyone's attention after they succeeded in smashing through the door. The detective hurried over, Andrew following with cautious curiosity. He caught sight of Sandra O'Reilly lying at the foot of Celia Braddock's stairs, looking above all things dead, her neck at a strange angle. He saw the soles of the feet of someone else, whom he assumed to be Celia, at the top of those stairs, but at this point the police ushered him away. Realising that this might have seemed abrupt, the detective, middle-aged, the weariness of his features shaken into life by the mystery of Merryking Close, gave a supportive pat on Andrew's shoulder before directing him back to his house.

Andrew paused at his door and looked up and down the Close, unable to shake the feeling that the events of the previous Monday night had played a huge part in all of that violent destruction. He wondered whether the detective might have been so benevolent to him if he knew of the non-disclosure agreement, which would have guaranteed the silence of all the players of that fateful game even before the Grim Reaper intervened. He contemplated telling the officers, but not for long. To his shame, he just shook his head and went inside, knowing of twelve million reasons why he would try to hold his tongue.

*

The December sunlight was already fading as the detective wandered back into Celia Braddock's hallway. He addressed the pathologist, who was in the process of screwing up his disposable overalls.

"You done already?"

"Yup, seems cut and dried," the pathologist looked faux-apologetic, "if you'll pardon the expression."

"And this is the murder weapon?" He pointed to a glass pumpkin, sitting on a table in the hallway and bent to look at it closely.

The pathologist's tone was drier than old bones. "Old woman's face smashed by a heavy object, traces of her blood, mucus and tissue on the glass, wound matches the dimensions – seems a fair initial assessment. I'm sure fingerprints will bear this out." He continued with his packing up. "She certainly wasn't hit with a real pumpkin."

"I think we have a rare one here." The detective looked around the hallway in an absent-minded way.

"You don't say. A row of three houses in an exclusive little road, each containing a dead body, five in total, just days after we were here because of a suicide across the road."

"Even the estate agents might be pushed here!"

"Do you think they're connected – the suicide at Number Three and all this mayhem?"

The detective pushed his hands further into his pockets and pulled a face. "It's got to be possible. But what I was referring to is that I think our little *objet d'art* may be the cause of this murder in more ways than one." He jerked a thumb towards Sandra O'Reilly's house. "The...presumed killer collects these things and having just had a look in her home, there's a coach missing from her Cinderella tableau. I can't imagine she brought it over here with murder aforethought. I shouldn't laugh..." He paused and did exactly that. "...but I think this'll be known as the Collectibles Murder, though heaven knows how anyone could get that angry over such things."

"Or excited." The pathologist's tone remained cynical. "So what will they call the others?" He gestured with his eyes down the Close in the direction of Brad Llewellyn's house.

"Fuck knows – madness? That one seems, as you would put it, cut and dried too, doesn't it? Fingerprints, DNA, and mud in all the right places." He gave a weary smile. "If only everything were so simple."

He headed back out into the Close and stood for a while, watching the winter shadows fall, trying to imagine what insanity had taken hold of those people in that exclusive little road.

CHAPTER 11

That evening, following a day of gruesome discoveries, Andrew Hansen opened his bedroom window, leaned out and looked up and down the street of horrors that was Merryking Close. His ensuing shudder had nothing to do with the December wind, which caused the striped tape around the neighbouring doors to flutter and rattle. He knew there were squad cars at either end of the Close. Now he took in the houses across the way. Each of them had witnessed violent death within the previous twenty-four hours. Crime scene barrier and door tape marked them out as being charnel houses instead of homes. Through the openings in the walls that gave the road its seclusion he could see no lights, people, or cameras, but there were voices, perhaps residents of nearby streets, or the press.

Puffing out his cheeks, he turned away and closed the windows, then forced himself to return to the task of packing. Having decided that he could not spend that night in the Close – in fact he wasn't sure whether he could ever live there again – he wanted to get away without having to run the gauntlet of the media. For more than one reason, he did not want them poking around in his life right now. Luckily it seemed the police had managed to keep any journalists at arm's length. He would need to sneak out somehow to speak with the officers so they could help him get away.

He froze for a moment. How exactly did the police view him in all of this? As an innocent party, the possibility that he might be under suspicion hadn't even crossed his mind – until now! Under the circumstances, he had to wonder – as the only survivor of that apocalyptic night, was he not only a suspect, but the prime one? Given the whole Chancery thing, it wasn't just the journos whose noses he needed to keep out of his private affairs.

His doorbell rang. There was an immediate chill in his veins, the product of a guilty conscience allied with an imagination that might have been considered over-active on a less surreal night. It had to be the police, given how tight the security was around the street.

He opened the window again, leaned out a little and saw Yvonne Elmer standing there, still in her business suit and carrying a briefcase. Sighing with relief, he hurried down and opened the door.

"What's going on?" she asked, dispensing with pleasant-ries, looking back down the Close at the policemen, then across at the demarcated houses. "I've just been asked by the police to provide identification. They said that they had tried to contact me at my place of work, but I was out with a client today…in Scotland. There was a missed call, but it was late and I didn't recognise the number." She gestured towards the men in uniform. "They said that there was nothing to worry about, but I would do best to come to you before I go into my house." She was wide-eyed and pale; she pointed towards the tape around the doors opposite. "Nothing to worry about! Andrew, what's happened?"

He urged her inside with a gesture, staying back from the door, just in case zoom lenses were already trained on it. "Thank God you're okay. They wanted to break down your door," he ushered her through, "but I told them your car wasn't there, so you were probably at work." That stopped her in her tracks. "Come in, come in. I'll pour us both a drink. It's quite a story."

*

If Yvonne had been pale before, she was a ghost now as Andrew finished recounting the day's events. From time to time she raised her hand to her throat in an involuntary gesture. "My God, it's like something from a horror movie or one of those...sci-fi things about mass hysteria or...I dunno, I don't know what I'm talking about." She took another large swig from the glass of whisky Andrew had given her. Suddenly she looked up, shocked. "Ever since we played that game. Do you think there was some power after all in Arthur's curse?" She downed the rest of the drink and Andrew refilled the glass.

"In that case Yvonne, none of you has...should have had anything to fear because you didn't win."

"You're right", she said, the relief evident in her voice. Then she realised what she had done and looked shamefaced.

"Having said that, everyone else who played has died..." he trailed off. "I'm so sorry – money clearly hasn't bought me brains. I didn't mean to scare you either."

"Actually, I didn't play."

He nodded in acknowledgement. "Very true – not that that excuses me." He smiled. "Then truly you have nothing to worry about."

Now Andrew walked across to the window and looked out on the scene while Yvonne responded: "Anyway, I withdrew for reasons of self-preservation, which hardly qualifies me for the 'holier than thou' award."

Andrew stayed with his back to Yvonne and continued to stare out at the lamp-lit Close. "But it's pretty obvious that there is a strong connection with the game."

Yvonne wandered across to join him. She placed a sympathetic hand on his shoulder, leaving Andrew to contemplate how, even in the darkest of places, the touch of a woman had its own powers. "You know, while we sat there, in Stoehlheim's boardroom, I remembered how, during my pupillage, the chamber used to celebrate a big case win with a bottle or two of wine and a game of Chancery. The resulting embarrassment, sometimes ill-feeling, was often huge...and that was without loaded questions."

"Arthur knew that we are all diseased, with itches that need scratching, scabs that need picking, boils that need lancing. His whole fortune was built on that precept."

"Your fortune now."

He ignored the interruption, which seemed a little crass. "And who had more time to observe us than him, sitting alone in that house, day in day out, year in year out?

"Celia Braddock?" There was light humour in Yvonne's tone and Andrew felt the merest of smiles tugging at the corner of his mouth for the first time in many hours.

"True! I wish I could say 'God rest her soul', but I can't." He thought for a moment. "But does Arthur deserve any better? Part of me thinks yes..." He paused. "...and not because I won his money, but because of his loneliness."

"You don't think Celia was lonely?"

Andrew stared at Number Four and gave a little nod. "Fair point - perhaps." He sipped at his own drink now. "I guess you could argue that her venom was at least spat out during her life, whereas Arthur..." He paused, lost in thought. "He has proved as lacking in compassion as his victims. He will have watched where we were vulnerable." Andrew smiled ironically. "Funny how we were lacking in humanity, yet ultimately proved to be all too human."

Now he turned at last to look at her. "Fair play to you, Yvonne. You didn't succumb, though at the end of the day, only you know why." Andrew took a sip of his drink and eyed her over then rim of his glass. Though she held his gaze, she looked a little awkward. "I'm guessing your secret is safe now." He turned back to the window. "And so are one or two others. God knows what that whole thing with Sandra and Celia was all about. Whatever it was, they're all past caring now."

"Well, as for me, as I said, I withdrew for very existentialist reasons of self-preservation, believe me. I'm sure our lawyer friend's poorly veiled threats about my career didn't escape you." Her next words were tinged with nervousness. "Have you gone to the police with any of this...about the game, I mean?"

Andrew gave her a guilty look. "I haven't," he sighed. "As I said, we're all human, Yvonne. I have just become secure financially for life. Nobody needs to know. I want to keep it quiet, though I'm sure it will come out somewhere, somehow. Arthur had no surviving family. I hate to admit that a large part of me doesn't want to give up the money now. I'll make sure that I try to do good with it as well. Please believe me; I have agonised over this, but in the battle with my conscience I have been fighting under a flag of convenience."

Yvonne took another large swig of whisky and sounding slightly slurred said: "You've lost me." She laughed, gesturing with a sweeping movement of the hand over her head.

"An A4-sized flag. I mean that I have taken the line of least resistance and I think I'm guilty of using the NDA as an excuse. Stoehlheim—"

"What do you make of him?" she interjected.

"You don't want to know. 'There are more things in heaven and earth...'" He trailed off, leaving the quote unfinished.

Once more Yvonne laughed, but this time there was an edge of frustration in the sound. "You've lost me again."

"Let's just say that whatever I feel about him, I wouldn't feel comfortable voicing it. Sounds daft, I know."

"Not at all. I know absolutely what you mean." Yvonne looked into a distant shadow somewhere. "I felt his power when I tried to leave the other night." She returned to the here and now. "Speaking of which, I should leave now." She put a hand on his arm. "I've kept you from whatever you were doing. Thank you for your time and the drink...drinks."

"Don't be silly – stay." Andrew felt a slight blush warm his face.

"I need to get going." She sounded a little unconvincing. "Would you mind seeing me back to my place? I don't think the Close will ever feel the same."

"Of course."

Yvonne started to button her jacket, but her fingers were clumsy and she gave a little giggle. "What did you put in my whisky?"

"A few too many top-ups." She smiled and headed towards the lounge door. Andrew reached out, put a hand on her shoulder to stop her, turned her. "Look, what I was doing before you arrived was packing. I'd decided I wasn't going to spend the night here, so I know exactly how you feel. How's about I come with you while you collect a few things and you stay here the night? I'm sure we could use each other's company." Now he blushed. "Oh, I meant the spare room of course."

She looked at the hand on her shoulder and placed her own on his, smiling.

*

They sat together on the sofa, more whisky in their glasses, their knees touching as they talked. Yvonne had changed from her business suit into jeans and a jumper. She gave a little laugh: "My apologies – what were you going to say earlier about Stoehlheim before I so rudely tried to leave?"

"After you had all gone last Monday – and thank you, by the way, for your hand of support then..." He noticed something fleeting in her eyes. "...well, it was the strangest thing."

"What?"

"Stoehlheim presented me with a copy of Arthur's will. It was in a sealed envelope. Get this – it already had my name on it as the sole beneficiary."

Yvonne frowned. "But what about...what did he read out before the game?"

"Exactly! It wasn't a will after all. I remember him saying it outlined Arthur's last wishes, but he used some other term."

"A makeshift will, I think." Yvonne looked angry.

"Anyway, I take your point – what was that whole charade, or to choose the correct game, Chancery, all about?"

"Perhaps Stoehlheim wrote your name into the document afterwards."

"No, you're not listening – I saw him produce it from his safe in a sealed envelope."

"So the whole evening was a sham." There was some petulance in Yvonne's tone. She got to her feet, a little unsteadily, arms folded across her chest as she paced around.

"Actually, I think the whole evening was about this." Andrew pointed towards the window, more particularly towards the houses beyond it. "I just don't know whether Arthur intended to be quite so spectacularly, horribly successful."

"And we were just pawns in his, or Stoehlheim's, strategy."

"Strange just how many images of games we use in our lives." His comment was lost on Yvonne, whom he guessed was running something through the litigious chambers of her mind, judging by her expression.

"So what do you think would have happened if someone else had won on Monday night?"

"This is said without a hint of arrogance, but I don't think that anyone else was ever going to win. And that is why I don't subscribe to the idea of being cursed. You remember that Arthur spoke of there being one exception to his curse? I have to now assume he meant me, but if he had already planned somehow that I would win the money – God knows how! – then no-one else could ever be the victim of his evil eye. There's an essential contradiction in that." Again he gestured towards the horrors beyond his window. "So what was all that about? It's self-inflicted madness."

"But how could that be?"

Andrew spread his hands wide and shrugged. There was so much he wanted to say in response, yet so little that made any sense, especially to him. "Maybe it was that Christmas card I sent him – but then I never took him up on his invitation for a drink, so why would I deserve better than anyone else?"

"No, I meant how could it be that you definitely won? This has to be illegal." She paced up and down, her index finger tapping on her chin, deep in thought. Andrew could see he had been right – for the moment Yvonne had forgotten that she was talking to the recipient of a vast fortune. She was thinking with her horsehair wig on, though it had been placed there in a mood of affronted personal and professional pride. "We could build a case here."

Her line of thought seemed selfish to Andrew. "Are you really going to take him on...Stoehlheim? And on what grounds? That he provoked everyone into killing each other?"

Or themselves – he paused for thought – *poor Darren*.

Yvonne stopped pacing. "Why not? Conspiracy to commit murder. It would be his word against all of us!"

Andrew pointed again towards the street. "Meaning just you and me, babe." He looked long at her and gave an ironic laugh.

"Look, he's just a solicitor."

"Is that all he is?

"What do you mean?" she asked with more than a little testiness.

"For someone who knows the devil..." Andrew closed his eyes for a split second and smiled, "...is in the detail, you have a short memory. You just mentioned his threats. I saw the look on your face when he confronted you. He scared you."

"No."

"Oh come on. He scared everyone, including me. I don't want to go up against him."

"That's easy for you to say; you have the money."

So, they had come to it at last. "Yes, but you can have it...if you really don't believe in ghosts and curses." It did occur to Andrew that Yvonne's beliefs would play no part in where the money was staying. Once again, just like that very morning as he had stepped out into the Close, he found himself wandering towards the moral high ground.

Nevertheless, Andrew got to his feet and that seemed to signal to Yvonne that she had overstepped the mark. She took a breath, crossed the room and extended her hand towards his arm. He backed away slightly.

Yvonne sighed. "Stoehlheim is powerful. Look, he's got us at it now." She stepped forward again. "I'm sorry, I think I'm still in a state of shock about it all."

She seemed to be backtracking, hoping the door hadn't closed behind her. Whether he was completely convinced or not, Andrew chose to leave it ajar. "That's okay. Look, if it's any consolation, I went over the same ground myself," he said, pulling a face, "though for more selfish reasons."

Andrew gestured Yvonne towards the sofa and they sat again. "Whatever way you look at it, Stoehlheim has covered his tracks. Remember how he collected up all the invitations? Never mind the non-disclosure agreement – now there's no proof that last Monday night ever happened. Apart from you and me, there are certainly no witnesses. No-one from the firm itself was there. There are legal documents to support my inheritance and not once in them is there any mention of it having been up for grabs to the winner of a game. And I would bet all of my newly acquired fortune on there being no trace left of Arthur Du Fuss's letters or that Chancery board."

All at once, Yvonne's features softened and she smiled. "You're absolutely right of course. I am sorry for having been irrational."

"I'm not sure there is a rational way to behave at this time." He paused for both thought and effect. "Except perhaps to have another drink?"

Yvonne shook her head and held her glass out anyway for Andrew to fill. He giggled and she followed suit. Then they both burst out laughing.

"Why are we laughing?" asked Yvonne.

"I believe it's called comic relief."

They regained their composure. Now Yvonne said: "Interesting that you referred to 'the firm'. Word gets around in law circles, yet I had no idea the other night when I arrived at Stoehlheim's office what was going on – and you know what..." she leaned conspiratorially towards Andrew, her face close to his, "...I have no idea who the other Stoehlheim is."

"The other Stoehlheim?"

"Yes, 'Stoehlheim and Stoehlheim'." She parenthesised in the air. "I don't know anyone who has ever met the other partner." They contemplated her words. Now Yvonne took another gulp of whisky – and then frowned in a way that marked a complete tangent in her thought process. "Andrew, what exactly was your answer to the final question the other night?"

He looked up, taken aback, not by the question, but by his mind's vague response to the challenge. "You know, I'm actually not sure. I seem to have only faint recollections of the whole incident from the moment all hell broke loose. I do remember putting my hand on the palm print, but I was..."

What the fuck!? There was a sudden dizziness. He didn't know what was happening, but became aware Yvonne had sat up straight and was looking at him with concern. "Andrew, are you OK? You've gone very pale."

He gave a horrified whisper: "My God, how could I have forgotten?"

Andrew is sitting in his place by the Chancery board – no-one else is. There are the raised voices of the other players arguing, but something else has caught Andrew's gaze and he cannot look away – something shimmering in the cage in the middle of the board. The protesting voices fade into the background. The shimmering condenses into the figure of Arthur Du Fuss. Andrew stares at it. Arthur approaches the bars of the miniature cage. His hands grasp them. There is a sound that might be the parallel world of man on the opposite bank of the river that separates him from death. Now another sound reaches Andrew's ears, faint, yet definable as cackling laughter, mixed with distant screams, but lost in another time and place to the ears of the living. Arthur looks over his shoulder towards some point from which the sounds seem to emanate. When he turns back to Andrew, the horror in his eyes makes the young man shudder.

Arthur reaches a hand through the bars towards him. "They are coming, looking for me. Limbo is not simply God's waiting room, young Andrew...it is also the Devil's. They are looking for me, his servants. They are looking for my soul."

There is a skin-crawling howling. Arthur sinks to his knees while Andrew watches horrified and continues in a choking whisper: "Only with prayers can the soul be saved. You are my only hope, young Andrew, which is as I planned. Ignore that card you are holding and answer me this." His face turns sad and full of despair. "Will you pray for my damned soul?"

Almost trance-like, Andrew places his hand on the Bible. "Yes." The Bible glows green.

"Thank you."

Arthur's face fades away. The howling and cackling fade with him. The protesting voices grow louder again. Silence – then there is a gasp, followed by the voice of Stoehlheim: "I believe we have a winner."

Andrew opened his eyes. He turned to find a thoughtful Yvonne looking at him. She placed a hand on his. "What happened, Andrew?"

He decided against the truth, for reasons that both escaped him and made sense: "I tried, but I have only faint recollections. I do remember putting my hand on the palm print; next thing, all hell's breaking loose."

"In a manner of speaking."

He paused, shrugged. "When I was in his office, Stoehlheim told me I had won because Brad read out my question.

Perhaps if you don't read out the question, you cannot lie. I don't know."

All he knew for certain was that he was lying now. What he had remembered was not something you shared.

Taking him by surprise, Yvonne leaned over and kissed him on the cheek. He felt his body respond; the breath from her words as she kept her lips close to his ear sent tingles through him. "I wish you well."

*

Andrew lay in his bed, looking at the light that fell from the street lamp through the open curtains. He became aware of the sound of feet padding along the landing from the spare room. His door opened gently and Yvonne entered, speaking soft words: "Like you said, it's just you and me, babe."

She climbed into his bed.

"And Biggles." He pointed. It was a throwaway line to cover his embarrassment. Yvonne looked towards the corner of the room where Biggles lay asleep in a basket.

"He won't mind."

Nor will I!

She cuddled up to Andrew, placed her lips on his. He responded with a passion that surprised him. Their love-making and later the sound of Biggles snoring in the corner of the room almost made him feel safe.

*

He might have felt less so if, instead of then falling asleep, he had seen the twist in Yvonne's features that settled at last on being a smile as she lay with her head on his chest, the lamplight reflecting eerily in her eyes while the police tape continued to flap in the gathering storm.

CHAPTER 12

Not for the first time in his recent history, Arthur woke with a start and his eyes flew open. From instinctive memory he put hands to head, where his fingertips felt solid bone and whole flesh. Probing and feeling, it seemed that everything was where it should be. His heartbeat thundered in his ears and he was drenched in sweat. As he pushed himself into a sitting position, the sumptuous but worn leather sofa on which he found himself squeaked and rumbled. Then he waited for the mists of disorientation to clear.

At length he bowed his head in relief before looking up again. The landmarks that came into view around him were unfamiliar at first, but through them he was able to piece together something of what must have happened to him. To his left on a long table stood a rank of six computer monitors with older-style glass screens which had seen better days; behind them on the wall hung a Miro abstract, the subject's one recognisable human eye discomfiting him. On the right-hand wall was a large plain mirror, placed there presumably to compensate for the room's lack of windows.

The memories were returning and as they condensed, so the claustrophobia of his dream lessened, though it could not diffuse completely in the windowless chamber. He had a vague recollection of starting to feel faint.

Where had he been? Ah yes, yes! The solicitor's office. Stoehlheim. He had gone to see him. He frowned as he remembered the reason for his visit to the law firm, though there was a contradictory and frustrating lack of recall.

Standing, he found that his legs were weak and shaky. The dream and then his awakening in the strange sterility of these surroundings were exhausting him.

Arthur looked around again, puffing out his cheeks. He must have passed out and someone, he presumed Stoehlheim, appeared to have brought him through into a training room of some sort to lie down. Just as well. Just as well. It was coming back to him now. Perhaps it had been God's way of stopping Arthur from proceeding along the road to Hell.

There was a door in the corner of the room to Arthur's right. He went across and opened it with caution. The cold air that enveloped him left him in no doubt that it led to Stoehlheim's office. The man clearly liked to stay alert. Across the room, the lawyer stood by his desk. His large frame was stooped over his computer monitor. The flickering images on the screen threw his features into spooky relief. There appeared to be some sort of activity on there, rather than two dimensional images, as if he was watching rather than reading. Arthur stood in the doorway, allowing the air conditioning to cool the sweat on his body.

Though he did not seem to have heard the door open above the hum of the aircon unit, Stoehlheim must have been alert to some minute change in the air. As he glanced over his shoulder, there was a momentary flicker of annoyance, or maybe surprise, in his eyes, which appeared for a second or two to have no whites. He passed his hand in a graceful but swift gesture across the screen, which went blank. Arthur assumed it had to be some state-of-the-art equipment, with sensors instead of switches.

Now the lawyer turned and advanced across the room towards him.

"I've changed my mind," said Arthur. Stoehlheim didn't break stride and Arthur felt panic rising, but continued with a touch of desperation, as if finishing what he wanted to say would halt Stoehlheim's advance. "I wish to change my instructions." He tried to hold his ground, but couldn't help backing away a bit.

Stoehlheim stopped in front of him, seeming to tower over him. "I am afraid it is a little late for that." He looked into the room behind Arthur, who turned and followed his gaze.

All but one of the six computer monitors had flickered into life. Each one displayed a similar, but slightly different pale image, set against a backdrop blacker than a bottomless pit on a moonless night.

Stoehlheim placed a firm, irresistible hand on Arthur's shoulder and turned him. They stepped back into the room of screens. Arthur squinted at them and then his eyes widened as he saw things on those monitors that chilled his heart to almost glacial stillness

The shapes on the screens were growing larger, familiar, yet incapable of finding their place ever again in the world of man. The pale images were the figures of his erstwhile neighbours, or at least some of them. From their hollow pupils he could tell that they were in complete darkness, despite the peculiar light reflecting off their skin. Those eyes looked around in jerky desperation, as if seeking something, some glimmer on which to anchor, but finding nothing. Now some of them were backing away again. Arthur could see, in the first screen, Brad Llewellyn groping into the blindness of the dark with one hand, while the other probed a jagged, dry wound in his stomach. He appeared to be saying something, but there was no sound.

On another screen blackness spreading like an inkblot transformed into the mouth of Emma Thomas.

"No!" That one hoarse syllable from Arthur's lips encapsulated the horror where a million words would have failed. It was almost a misplaced echo, because Emma's mouth had opened in a silent scream. Nothing showed in that gaping hole, not even the faintest of reflections off tooth or tongue. Now her hands went to her face. She looked around her in terror and it was clear that she was screaming again. There was a horrible familiarity in the image and indeed, Stoehlheim gestured back towards his office, saying: "Edvard Munch owes me a great deal." He laughed, a sound devoid of all humanity.

"No!" Again, it was all Arthur could find to say and all that needed saying. He turned his head away and squeezed his eyes shut.

"Yes – indeed yes." Stoehlheim's response was also perfect in its succinctness. He placed a vice-like grip on Arthur's head, turning it back towards the screens. "Observe your work."

Almost beyond belief, there was worse to see. The thing that probed its misshapen, mutilated non-face with desperate, gnarled fingers appeared to be Celia Braddock, her eyes turned in towards the smashed socket where a nose should have been. Another screen revealed Sandra O'Reilly holding her hands to her head as she searched the void, but each time she let go to reach out into the darkness, grasping at an unimaginable something, her unsupported head lolled at grotesque, impossible angles...as indeed did the head of Darren Thomas, though he was further impaired by bulging eyes and a swollen, protruding tongue, which he attempted, from time to time, to push back into his mouth, though it flopped back out in repeated defiance.

Arthur could take no more of these nightmarish visions and sank to his knees, dread, terrible comprehension and desperate denial churning in his stomach. He retched, fought the resulting bile and whispered: "What horrible trick is this?"

Stoehlheim merely stood at the side of him and said: "No trick, Arthur Du Fuss. You know it is no trick. I have merely brought you where you wanted to be."

"Please stop it!"

"That is, if not beyond my powers, then against the laws of Creation." Arthur looked up in slow comprehension at him and the lawyer nodded. "Yes, Arthur, they are dead.

And they are some of the lucky ones. At least they have their injuries and malformations to distract them once in a while. Others who have done wrong and have sinned simply die in their sleep, physically whole. Imagine that." Acidic sarcasm dripped from those last two words.

Arthur put his hands over his face, both understanding and denying everything. "Oh my God! You taunt and torment me."

"An ironic imprecation, but more accurate than you know. It is certainly not me who created the laws governing this universe."

Arthur started to sob, his words breaking on his shuddering breaths. "What will become of them? I don't understand."

"Yes, you do," Stoehlheim paused for effect, "only too well. They are in what mankind likes to refer to as Hell, though not as he has ever pictured it. Nothing will become of them. And what greater punishment, what worse torture could there be than this void? There are no Dante-esque levels to descend here, no goading demons with tridents, no scorching flames nor eternal backbreaking labour, or whatever means man has used during his pitifully short history to try to comprehend and capture the concept of hopelessness without end." Now Stoehlheim placed a hand on Arthur's shoulder. He flexed his fingers, causing Arthur to yelp with pain as he tried, but failed to break away from the iron claws. "Ah yes, pain – it would be a relief in the purity of its sensation."

He released Arthur, who slumped. Stoehlheim approached the screens and gestured towards them. It seemed Arthur would be spared nothing of the consequences of his actions.

"They are condemned to wander for all eternity in a soundless world. The silence is total. They cannot even hear themselves scream. There is sound on these computers and they are set at maximum volume. This is definitely a program with WYSIWYG, Arthur. Touch and smell are denied them. There is no light. Even their wounds give no pain. Theirs is a world of nothingness, forever. It is only through our, shall we say, unique position here that we are able to see them. But they remain sentient beings, enough at least to fulfil the purpose of their Hell."

"I don't want to see them anymore," wailed Arthur, pressing his face deeper into his hands.

Stoehlheim adopted a theatrical tone, for the stage was his. "Such a contrary creature is man – you condemned them for the very reason that you never saw them." Now he paused for effect. "Hard, is it not – to see what you always wished for; to look on all you created and see that it is not good?" He grinned at his play on the opening of Genesis and his next words were laced with irony. "Imagine how God feels! Small wonder that man has been abandoned."

Arthur was sobbing, but Stoehlheim continued. There was no hand of comfort for the snivelling wretch at his feet. He leaned almost lazily on one of the computers and pointed to it. "Behold, Arthur Du Fuss, for this is your gift to them in perpetuity – and they deserve it. For did they not leave you feeling like a man cut off from life?"

"No!" Arthur slumped forward until his forehead rested on the floor. His sides heaved, wracked by rasping breaths.

"You will need to come up with something different from now on. Eternity might drag if that one response is your only offer." Stoehlheim looked down at him and sneered. "Ah, a weeping and a wailing and a gnashing of teeth. Listening to you, I think that aforementioned silence is preferable after all."

Now Stoehlheim stepped towards Arthur again, his feet by the prostrate man's head. A chill seemed to descend over Arthur, who looked up through his tears and suddenly, recognising that self-pity would be his only consolation, found enough courage to respond to the taunting figure that loomed over him. "Why are you doing this? And what did you mean by eternity? What is to become of me?"

"It would be more correct to ask what has become of you. Come, Arthur Du Fuss."

Stoehlheim extended a hand, which in his weakness Arthur took out of necessity. The lawyer led him across to the mirror. Arthur's legs buckled as he saw that he had no reflection. Even in the extremity of his shock, he noticed that the reflected monitors bore no images on their screens. He turned, but the horrific dumb shows were still in place, the figures getting smaller as they stumbled onwards in their infinite black void. He turned back to Stoehlheim, pleading and helpless. "I don't understand."

"The mirror merely reflects the room as others would see it if they were to enter now." Stoehlheim put a finger thought-fully to his lips and walked away from Arthur towards the door of his office. "You see, Arthur, I don't quite know how to break this to you, but you are a little bit..." He turned, his blazing eyes a reflection of every horror he had ever seen, teeth sharp, lips thin and cruel and the voice an abomination. "DEAD!"

Arthur's hands flew to his face again to shield his eyes from this vision. He heard Stoehlheim speak, and when he dared to look, the lawyer was himself again, standing shaking his head, big and powerful, his body throwing a huge shadow on the wall behind him that seemed to pulse with some force of its own as he continued:

"Still the same pathetic, snivelling, self-pitying wretch that you were five centuries ago."

"I don't understand."

"You do love to repeat yourself."

Stoehlheim moved with tangible malevolence towards him, causing Arthur to flinch. He put his hand on the collar of Arthur's shirt and lifted him clean off the floor, before setting him down again with a thump, leaving him to choke a few deep breaths of recovery, while he continued. The voice remained rasping and sibilant, growing more powerful and menacing, while the shadow on the wall appeared to have thickened. The old man quailed before him, any vestiges of frail courage gone.

"First it was knowledge and power I gave you." Stoehlheim gave a dismissive click of his fingers. "These you wasted, as I knew you would. But you were spared, and my place is..." He paused. "...was not to question. Centuries later you were given another chance." Stoehlheim held

Arthur's gaze. "Then your wife died." The lawyer shot Arthur a knowing look and raised his hands. "Such are the sick ways of the one to whom you all run in your hour of need, though in reality you, mankind, are merely running away from yourselves and the consequences of your actions. But even you recognised that he had abandoned you, because to me you came once again, and this time there was no going back. I listened when you said that you would give anything to be with her again."

Arthur's eyes widened. "Listened? But I am lost and still without her."

"Exactly – I said *listened*. There is never any going back, on one's actions or to one's past. Instead, I gave you the wealth and the means, through the extraordinary success of our joint venture, Chancery, to destroy those who offended you." Stoehlheim stroked his chin for a moment and appeared distracted. His voice softened and returned to the mesmer-ising, powerful timbre that the courts of the world knew so well. "Yes, a remarkable success, that Chancery. We can be proud of ourselves." He turned back to Arthur. "And that is where we find ourselves today. This time the door is closed. Time to move on."

"What door? I..."

"How could you, of all people, forget that there would be a price?"

Stoehlheim's shadow returned to its human dimensions and he set off again towards his office while Arthur strug-gled to his feet. "Wait, please wait." Stoehlheim stopped.

"You talked just now as if I had a life before this one? Who was I? And where am I now? There is much I need to know."

Stoehlheim laughed. It was not a cruel sound, but one full of irony. "That is rich coming from you, who had a world of knowledge at your fingertips so long ago, courtesy of me."

"What do you mean?"

"Enough. No more questions. A dead man is not entitled to any answers." Then Stoehlheim touched his chin, as if considering something. "Let us just say, if you had read more, certain things might have rung a distant bell. Now is too late."

Arthur turned and forced himself to look at the screens again.

Stoehlheim watched him. "I see their pain in your eyes, Arthur."

The old man nodded as he looked at the diminishing white figures. He could see now that all of them were crying out in their desperation. He was forced for a moment to question whether he still had a heart, because it seemed to be aching as they groped onwards, and for Emma Thomas in particular. "What have I done? What have I caused through my pride? They have committed no crimes."

Now Stoehlheim was at Arthur's shoulder, the movement so swift that his voice in his ear startled him. "So typical of man's arrogance. He searches and thinks that he discovers, dissects, seeking the inner workings and the mechanics of everything he encounters, and sees nothing. He plans to probe the outer reaches of the universe. If he ever gets there, he will wish that he had not, because his pitiful mind will not comprehend what it finds. Let me correct your statement before we go any further." The lawyer's eyes seemed to achieve the impossible, as if darkness could blaze. "At least two of these lost souls have committed murder. You saw it all, Arthur, in what you thought was a dream, yet you judge only from mankind's perspective."

Stoehlheim crossed to the screens. He walked along, pointing to them appropriately as he spoke, sometimes returning to one, his fingernail making a hollow ring as he tapped on the glass: "Thou shalt not kill; thou shalt not commit adultery; thou shalt not kill; thou shalt not commit adultery; thou shalt not bear false witness against thy neighbour; thou shalt not steal; thou shalt not covet thy neighbour's wife; nor anything that is thy neighbour's; thou shalt have no other gods before me; remember the Sabbath day, to keep it holy."

He walked across again to Arthur and pushed the same long finger against his chest. "And that is just the Commandments. I have not even touched upon the sins, one of which, pride, you rightly acknowledged as your own."

Arthur's mouth had fallen open. He stuttered: "But... but...those are just..."

Stoehlheim stood before him, drawing himself up while the air around him seemed to crackle. "Choose your next words with care, Arthur Du Fuss, for if you are about to dismiss the laws of the universe, then I must be a figment of your imagination." The lawyer leaned forward until his face almost pressed against Arthur's. The old man could feel the heat emanating from his skin. "And I assure you I am not."

Arthur remained silent. Too late he saw everything for what it was. Stoehlheim seemed to notice this and smiled with satisfaction. Then in a tone that was almost playful compared with what had gone before he said: "I believe I have developed a taste for playing games. So Arthur Du Fuss, I am going to say that those five souls have one last chance." Once again he placed a heavy hand on Arthur's shoulder. "And that chance is you."

Arthur's emotions were a toxic mixture of hope and dread.

The lawyer pointed. "You see that blank screen over there? That was reserved for you. At the moment, as a suicide, you are in what might best be described as 'Limbo'. I prefer to call it my waiting room." He laughed at his little joke. "Darren Thomas might have joined you, if he hadn't worked on Sundays." He paused for what seemed like comic effect. "Oh, and not committed a double murder." The frivolity of Stoehlheim's tone in the wake of such condemnation was disorientating. "But I digress. I would be prepared to release them all at your request."

Arthur stayed silent, so his host continued: "You disappoint me. I would have expected some word of thanks."

"I am merely waiting for the hammer to fall. Just as in life nothing comes from nothing, I assume the same applies in death."

Stoehlheim nodded his approval. "You have learnt quickly."

"Not quickly enough. I am too terrified to hope."

"Yes – better to shake that imposter from your shoulder. As a wise woman once said: 'I can take the despair – it's the hope I can't stand.'"

Stoehlheim paced across the room before continuing. "Well, yes, there would be a price naturally. You would have to take their place in that eternal darkness."

Stoehlheim appeared to be studying Arthur and added: "Is that hope I see on your shoulder again, despite my warning?"

"If it is, I suppose it would be a first for a dead man."

The lawyer gave a wolfish smile of acknowledgement. "I see you have started to develop gallows humour."

"It's strange the peculiar insightful moments that can be found in the eye of a storm. You cannot blame me for being hopeful when it seems an eternity of insensate darkness is not necessarily my fate." Stoehlheim merely shrugged and Arthur continued. "But would my replacing them not be going against those laws of Creation you mentioned?"

"Do you believe everything you are told?" That double-edged response was all the guidance he would get. Now Stoehlheim seemed to be growing impatient. "I would hurry, if I were you, Arthur. Your time is running out." He pointed and Arthur turned to find an hourglass he had not noticed before on top of a filing cabinet. There was little sand left in the upper glass. "However, I sense your decision is already made. As you said, their fate is not necessarily yours. Not feeling their pain quite so intensely now, I imagine." The last words stung – as they were meant to.

In response, Arthur felt some vestiges of defiance. "You haven't told me the alternative."

Stoehlheim gave a sigh of frustration. "You really still do not comprehend the fundamental laws, do you? But look at the images in those screens. Does it really matter what choice you have?"

Arthur felt aggrieved, being toyed with in death, perhaps more so because now he knew the same could be said of much of his life. Another pulse of belated, preternatural courage beat through him. "Humour an old man."

Stoehlheim tutted as if this was becoming tiresome. Then he gave a thin smile: "Very well, old man, who will come to realise that he does not know the meaning of 'old'. The alternative is that you will walk out of this building back into the world as you know it, but not as it knows you. You will remain in Limbo. Your presence will touch no-one. They will not feel you, nor you them. You will not be heard. You may walk the face of the earth, free to go where you please. The sun will not warm your blood, nor cold winds freeze your bones, for in reality you will have neither. You will hear things that amuse or distress you, but no-one will hear you laugh or cry. Séances will frustrate you immeasurably! The perfumes of flowers and women will pass you by. Food and drink will have no taste, but then again, you will have neither hunger nor thirst. In short, Arthur, you will be what is perhaps best described as a ghost, but no creature will ever know you are there. Once in a millennium, thanks to some peculiar conjoining of certain elemental forces, your presence may register as a chill down someone's spine or the raised hackles on a dog's back, but that will be it." A tear tracked slowly down Arthur's cheek. Stoehlheim pointed to it. "Save those, Arthur. They are merely the condensation of the last vestiges of the life you knew. Soon they will be dry."

"But I will be able to see and hear things."

Stoehlheim sighed again. "Not unless your apparent inability to listen disappears! That is part of the punishment: exclusion from everything that you see or hear."

Arthur straightened and wiped the back of his hand across his cheeks. "Well, I will take with me the hope that, even once in a thousand years, someone may feel I am there. And much as I regret what I have done..." Here he pointed to the screens. "...anything must be better than that."

"But do remember, Arthur, as the thousands of millennia drag past, you will survive it all and some of it you will not wish to see, for the destruction will not be undone quickly, if ever."

"I understand. And I will take that chance."

"So you condemn these others to their fates, giving them no chance to escape their darkness and utter unending despair?"

Arthur hesitated and then gave a slow nod. "There was a choice in my world, Mr Stoehlheim, known as Hobson's choice."

The lawyer also nodded and then extended his hand in the direction of the door. "In that case, it has been a pleasure doing business with you, Mr Du Fuss."

Arthur moved through the office towards the outer door. He glanced at Stoehlheim's computer and then came to an abrupt stop. "I am even more of a selfish fool than I thought," he said. Stoehlheim frowned. "I wish to ask another question." The lawyer – oh, how Arthur wished his host were merely that particular secular devil – pressed a strong hand into his back to guide him out of the office, but Arthur pointed to the hourglass and said, "I still have some time."

"That is time I granted you; it is not your right."

"I know what you were looking at now, on your computer when I first awoke. Two of them slipped through the net didn't they? Young Andrew Hansen and Yvonne Elmer. What will become of them?"

"Those were two questions, though I grant you one was rhetorical." Stoehlheim smiled and flicked his hand across the front of his computer. Gradually an image came into focus. A man and a woman lying in bed – Andrew and Yvonne – her head resting on his chest. Arthur smiled, but then looked at the aquiline, cruel features of the lawyer as he watched the screen and spoke.

"See how she smiles. I am a smile watcher. I can read her mind. They sought genuine comfort in each other and I think she actually likes him. But she cannot help her inclinations. She is thinking about the fortune. We know what a mighty aphrodisiac it can be to some people."

Stoehlheim blanked the screen again, turned to Arthur with an expression older than the hills and took him once more by the shoulder, leading him towards the door as he spoke: "She is the perfect vessel. There may be a marriage, perhaps a messy divorce. One of them is a lawyer; the other may need one. Mr Hansen has my card. Don't you worry, Arthur Du Fuss; it will be as it is meant to be..." He paused. "...for no-one slips through my net."

They passed through the outer office, which was in darkness save for the faint green stand-by lights from the non-diabolical computers. Stoehlheim opened the door and ushered Arthur out. He looked up and down the empty street. In the distance a lone car passed along the main road. A door closed. Arthur turned, and then turned again to face his new world.

CHAPTER 13

It was as if, with the closing of that door, Arthur's eyes opened for the first time to the reality. What the hell had he been thinking? What utter nonsense was this?

A faint thrumming told him of life on the distant motorway even at this early hour. There was birdsong. A robin hopped onto a gatepost and seemed to be looking at him, cocking its head, hopeful of its first meal of the day – one for which no effort was required. What wonderful symbolism, because Arthur realised now, that was exactly what he had been – a meal ticket.

Trees rustled in the shadows as if sniggering at him.

What a bloody fool! He had been so fixated on his need for revenge that he had lost all track of material and fact.

He turned and looked again at that wooden front door, which had closed behind him. Solid, oak, substantial. The only Hell lurking behind there was the everyday one known as a legal practice, that den of devils.

He saw now how simple this whole charade must have been to set up. When he had woken up in that back office, he hadn't questioned at all the fact of him resting in there and, of course, the administration of some sort of drug and a hallucinogen could have been responsible for that.

He lifted his hand to his head, just as he had on waking. There it was again – hard physical matter beneath his fingertips. He was no walking ghost. Offer a solicitor ten per cent of fourteen million pounds and he can afford the best software experts to set up something in his computer. Those dreadful visions of his neighbours in their individual Hells – very well done and terrible to behold; anything was possible nowadays. It dawned on him now why Stoehlheim had insisted on money up front.

Now panic set in. He wondered what exactly he had agreed to. The memories were sketchy. What had he signed? Where was the rest of the money? It hadn't been staked on a board game, winner takes all. That was nonsense – but what had he agreed?

He turned, meaning to knock on the door, but knew a charlatan like Stoehlheim – perhaps the word *charlatan* didn't do justice to the sophistication of his duplicity – would just refuse to answer. In some ways it did not matter; nothing would happen until he died anyway. In a moment of dark, almost humorous distraction, he wondered whether he should try to get hold of some of whatever it was Stoehlheim had administered. After all, the fantasy world of his recent hallucinations had to be preferable to his mundane existence. The visions of the last few hours could not alter the fact of a world without Helen and a life about which no-one else cared.

Whatever – he knew a good café in this part of town and that was where he would head now. Despite everything, his overriding emotion was one of relief. Hopefully, once his head had cleared, he would find out exactly what had gone on; reassess it all in the cold light of day.

He stopped in his tracks.

The cold light of day.

It wasn't the weather that made his blood slow now, but the thought of it. Perhaps it was also the crisp packet that had skittered past him as he had wandered from the side street onto the main road.

It was winter; there was a breeze, yet he felt neither chill nor wind-chill in the movement of air. He thought again of those rustling, sniggering trees.

What did filter into his consciousness was the onset of a touch of panic. No matter how far-fetched and unbelievable the events of the last hours, he was unable to shake off the threads and shards of discomfort.

He saw the café, a little way up the street. Despite the early hour, it looked open and busy. He remembered the few times he had called in; it seemed popular with long-distance lorry drivers and the lonely.

He needed to sit, place his hands around a cup of coffee – feel its reality.

He was struck now by a couple of things as he approached. Several of the tables outside were occupied, despite the early hour and the chill of December. Judging by their clothing, these guys were indeed lorry drivers or perhaps construction workers. Doubtless the drivers, after endless hours in their cabs, relished the freedom of the fresh air as they demolished bacon rolls. All of them looked as tough as nails and yet they were still wrapped in fleeces and coats, so once again Arthur was struck by his failure, as he saw it, to feel the cold, despite being clad in the smart-casual attire he had worn for his visit to Stoehlheim.

The other thing that threw him was not one of them looked up at him as he walked past; perhaps not unusual in itself, but then again, people were driven by innate curiosity, even nosiness.

There was a dog sitting by one of the tables, scrounging for scraps possibly; maybe the owner's dog. He paid no attention to Arthur. Yes, the draw of bacon rolls might have been that much stronger – no *might* about it. Arthur wanted to click his fingers, draw its attention. Something held him back. He remembered Stoehlheim's words:

"The sun will not warm your blood, nor cold winds freeze your bones...Once in a millennium, thanks to some peculiar conjoining of certain elemental forces, your presence may register as a chill down someone's spine or the raised hackles on a dog's back, but that will be it."

He walked on and pushed the door of the café. It swung open under his efforts, to his intense relief. That comfort was short-lived. Not a single person looked across at the door in absent-minded curiosity before returning to their drinks and conversations. Worse was the lack of reaction from the woman behind the counter, who continued to busy herself washing cups and throwing bacon on the hotplate. Even as she turned to face the café, Arthur's presence didn't seem to register. Perhaps she was just very rude, but he doubted that.

Which was when he remembered the mirror in Stoehlheim's training room.

He looked across at a wall to his left, doubtless mirrored to make the small dining area feel bigger. His absence from its reflections left little doubt of the huge void in which he now stood, a prisoner in its vast emptiness.

As he left the café now, he forced himself to picture the dreadful images of his former neighbours, shown to him minutes before by Stoehlheim. It was the only way he could deal with what lay ahead, the fact that he could at least see it and hear it. Even so, the memories taunted him, as he remembered the last time he had seen all of them alive, walking from their homes, unaware of him and the fate to which he would soon condemn them. What wouldn't he give to turn the clock back and be staring at them all from behind his net curtains, full of contempt and hurt, full of life?

*

He didn't recall much of the following hours, except that for now he still counted time in those tiny units and the city streets started to fill with lives. He didn't dare try to speak with anyone, to interact in any way. Here was Pandora's Box, the only question being whether he was inside or outside.

But the worst, for that day anyway, was still to come.

He was sitting on a bench near a main thoroughfare. If he had any lingering doubts about the cold truth of

Stoehlheim's words, they were blown away by the sight of a woman moving amongst the crowds, her expression of unutterable sadness almost certainly a mirror of his own. He called to her. No-one's head turned at the sound of his voice, including hers.

"Helen!"

She pushed on through the throng, head down. He rose from the bench and started to follow her, moving at last alongside her, at which point he realised – it wasn't Helen.

"I'm sorry," he said to her, a phrase that conveyed so much more than its constituent parts. She moved on, unaware of his presence.

Arthur couldn't help wondering whether this was a final twist of the knife, courtesy of Stoehlheim. It was now crystal clear, he was in Limbo and whatever one chose to believe, Helen couldn't be here. Nor could she be in that world, which it seemed was his to observe for as long as God and the universe deemed appropriate. Was this the lawyer simply reminding him how lonely he would be?

He forced himself once again to remember those ghastly, dreadful images in the computer screens just a short time before, to remind himself that, no matter what he went through here, it had to be better than the eternities facing those wretches.

Which was when fate played one final trick.

Helen had committed adultery. According to the laws Stoehlheim had expounded, there would be a personal Hell set aside for her.

Not for the last time, Arthur put his hands to his face and wept. There were tears, but they moistened neither his fingers nor his face.

He was about to learn that, even in Limbo, you could never forget.

*

Fifteen years before

He had waited until she was in the shower, called out his goodbye and then simply sneaked up into the attic – his den. Up there, he had tortured himself, picturing her under the flowing water making the garden rosy.

"But you are to blame," the imp on his shoulder had said. *"You've allowed the brambles to grow. No woman's going to love an obsessive engineer."*

That wasn't strictly true, of course. An engineer with enough zeroes on the correct side of the decimal point on the bank balance would always attract interest.

Of the wrong sort.

He had just wanted her to be patient; he knew the breakthrough was coming. Instead of which, he had arrived home mid-morning a few days before, having forgotten a couple of key documents for that day's work, and passed a rather suave guy in Merryking Close, whom he couldn't be sure hadn't just cut short a wave back towards Number Three. And had it been Arthur's imagination, or had the lounge curtains fallen back into place? All doubt was cast aside when he found Helen home, instead of at her tennis club.

Well, that had been a week ago – today was tennis club again and, in the meantime, he had been monitoring slight changes in her behaviour; a touch more secrecy about receiving texts, the phone beeping at strange times, and her tendency to take it with her around the house far more than she had.

Now he sat stewing, in all senses, in the attic, unable to switch on the air-conditioning unit for fear of the noise. Hearing a phone ring, for an awful moment he thought he had forgotten to put his on silent, but then he heard her speak. He couldn't make out what she was saying, partly because of the insulation in the loft but also because she seemed to be talking in a hushed voice, presumably the Pavlovian response of a guilty conscience, because after all, she believed she was alone.

Then the front door closed and there was nothing he could do but wait; caught in the perverse predicament of the eavesdropper – hoping he was wrong, hoping he was right.

He knew tennis club days would make the most sense for her, as they coincided with the Friday when Celia Braddock left her lair to do her weekly shop.

About three quarters of an hour later, there was the sound of a key in the lock downstairs, opening the door to demons. He heard a man's voice and felt the despair of vindication. It sounded like they were wandering through... *his* house. When he couldn't hear them, the air hissed with the whispering of the ancient Furies, trying to stoke vengeance, everything they uttered just variations of the same message: never mind him wandering through your house, soon he will be ploughing between her parted legs.

Arthur's face sank into his hands, a gesture he could not have known would become all too familiar to him.

Now, moving with stealth, trying to avoid any noise from the beams, he went to a corner of the loft, unlocked a trunk and removed the shotgun. He examined it, remembering the whim on which he had bought it at a flea market from someone with an Eastern European voice, who had several hidden in a crate beneath his stall, while he had been on a conference. He had purchased it as a beautiful piece of engineering, doubting he would ever use it.

The sounds of intimacy he was hearing now changed all that; her gasps and the groans from the man that spoke of reciprocity.

Recognising the creaking that followed as being from their bed, he exited the attic with silent care and stole through into the bedroom, the gun dangling in his fingers. As he stood there, he found a universal truth – it didn't matter what else happened, but the sight of your partner's eyes closed, their humanity gone, subsumed by physical intimacy with someone else...that sealed the deal, more than the crudity of fucking or sucking. A glance at the floor showed the dress she had discarded, a little black number, definitely not tennis attire!

The floor squeaked a warning beneath his tread. Her eyes opened. He enjoyed her horror, which equated to his power. For once in his life he held all the cards – although not according to that imp on his shoulder, which said: *"Yes, but you have lost her."*

He looked into her widening eyes, saw how she tried to push herself up the bed, away from her lover's probing mouth and how the latter misread those signals. In her widening pupils was a subset of passion, but not the one which had stared at him when they first kissed, when he proposed, when they married.

The noisy diner still seemed oblivious to the presence of the ferryman, even when Helen said: "Please...I'm so sorry!" He looked up, seemed puzzled, perhaps thinking she was having second thoughts. "I'm so sorry...please...!" Now his gaze followed hers and he threw himself back on the bed.

"So am I." It was all Arthur could think of to say, maybe because it was the absolute, succinct truth.

He lifted the twin barrels of the gun. Perhaps as an attempt to stop the worst, some sprite dug deep into the blackest recesses of Arthur's humour as he watched the other man's previously mighty weapon performing the opposite movement to the shotgun.

He pointed the gun at Helen – his unfaithful wife. There was a stillness deeper than the end of time and even emptier. Now Arthur realised he had closed his eyes. Opening them again, he saw neither of his victims had moved and were watching him with the stillness of statues. Such was the paradox of guilt – it had taken away their ability to run.

Still there were no words. At length, after squeezing his eyes shut once more and then shaking his head. Arthur dropped his arms and allowed the gun to hang useless in his fingers. Head still shaking, he walked from the bedroom and from the scene, presumably to their amazement, though he never stopped to check.

*

Looking back, he knew that he was lucky no-one was around that morning as he walked from the house and out onto the main street, shotgun in hand. He could only imagine how events might have panned out if someone had seen him. On reflection, things might have worked out better.

*

At last, he gathered himself together, opened the boot of his old, boxy Volvo and threw the shotgun in, before getting into the car and resting his forehead on the steering wheel. He didn't weep – there would be a time for that.

He could only imagine what Helen and her lover had said after he'd left – it can't have been much, under the circumstances! – and it was barely a couple of minutes until, from his position in the Volvo, Arthur watched the philanderer scuttle away, looking in all directions as he did so, presumably seeking the enraged husband, but not knowing Arthur's car.

*

He left it some hours before returning home. Helen was sitting in a plaid skirt and cardigan, penitential robes, with head bowed and fingers intertwined.

It was hard to believe – to take in – what he heard next – "Would you like a cup of tea?" – the more so because the words issued from his lips. They said everything that was right and everything that was wrong about being British.

Helen gave the merest nod of shame and didn't look up.

Because it suited him to do so, Arthur brought the tea in china-ware and took pleasure in the shaking of his wife's hand as she held the delicate cup and saucer. However, he noticed how his own hands betrayed him too. He needed that reminder. He wanted never to forget.

*

Some days passed in an uneasy truce and then Arthur decided that, at last, it was time.

"I think we should go out," he announced to Helen. To say the least, she looked taken aback.

"Out?"

They had barely ventured into the garden since that epiphany.

"I think it's time we put certain things behind us. Also, I have reason to celebrate – a work project of mine has been given the go-ahead. I'll show you what that's all about on our way to dinner."

He wandered over, took her by the hand, noticing the sweat on her palm as he helped her from her chair. As he led her upstairs, he became very aware of the symbolism this might have involved for her. Their making-up had not involved any physicality and that side of their relationship had, in any case, been dormant for years. How he hoped these moments were causing her discomfort. He might have tried to forget and move on, but he had not yet forgiven.

He led her into what had become her bedroom – no way could he have slept on those tainted sheets anymore – and caught the look in her eyes as she spotted the black dress laid out by him on the bed. She'd not worn it since...well, she hadn't worn it much before either. In fact, on reflection, he didn't remember buying it for her.

"*That's your bad,*" said the imp on his shoulder.

And, as she pulled it on, he saw the truth of that. He had been staring at figures on a board game instead of her figure and had reaped the whirlwind.

Once they were ready, after he had pulled on a jacket and smart trousers, they headed off in his car.

*

After a lengthy drive, she plucked up the courage to speak, something she hadn't managed without his prompting in the previous few days. He picked up that her question wasn't driven by mere curiosity, but a certain anxiety. "Where are we?"

It was not the most salubrious part of the city, for sure; one of those backwaters that can lurk behind the more vibrant parts of a town and can turn from seedy to trendy on a whim.

"Nearly there, sweetheart." He sensed how any term of endearment made her feel uncomfortable. Oh the irony of human existence, where a lack of passion could force someone to seek it elsewhere and the re-emergence of it in the previously fallow field became a nuisance; a crop you no longer wished to harvest.

Soon they drove past some unprepossessing blocks of flats and then, perhaps a mile further on, passed down a narrow lane to be met by wrought iron gates overgrown by weeds and nettles. He killed the lights.

"What is this place?"

Her voice trembled with doubt; he fed on that, placing a hand on her thigh and noticing her poor attempt to disguise the discomfort. "Don't worry, it's not as bad as it looks." He gestured through the windscreen. "I own this."

"You own...this?"

"Don't look so unimpressed. Real estate in the city is a sound investment. This is brown belt land."

"But why? I mean, if you had that money..." Too late, she realised what she was about to say and tried to stop herself, but he responded in a way that he could see surprised her.

"I know that I haven't been fair to you. I've been investing my money in the wrong place – except this now turns out to be the right place." He tilted his head.

Getting out of the car, he unlocked the gate and drove through, then returned to lock it again, while she watched him, frowning and intense "Oh, it's just to stop anyone following us in," he assured her. "What we have here is worth a lot of money." He drove on, the headlights still off. "It's securely fenced. Wouldn't want druggies or the homeless or such like thinking this might be a suitable meeting place."

He stopped the car and gestured for her to get out. Now he produced a torch from his pocket and lit the way across the urban wasteland. A little way ahead in the beam of the torch stood something that looked like a giant pile of cases, the sort used to carry bowling balls – cylindrical, but several feet in length.

"I don't understand." She folded her arms as if she was feeling the cold in her little black dress. "How is this going to be worth a lot of money?"

"This was a project of mine. It's based on a concept I observed in Japan some years ago." He gestured with his thumb towards the lights of the city in the semi-distance. "Something of potential use to people who are over there right now, living it up."

With that he removed a remote control from his pocket and pointed it towards one of the cylinders, which opened slowly to reveal a cushioned, lit interior; what looked like a bed, in fact. He signalled for her to move closer, sensed her tension and stepped ahead of her to put her mind at ease.

He pointed: "This, as you may have guessed, is a bed, this..." he pointed to a small white unit at the foot of the bed, "...is a little refrigerator for drinks, or water, or what-ever, and this..." he indicated some pipes along the interior of the lid, "...is your ventilation. If you've been on the pop all evening or, heaven forbid, need to lie low for a night or two, it's the perfect place to hide away."

"In that?" She pointed and her derogatory tone sealed her fate.

He continued: "It's soundproofed – in both directions," he smiled, "and no-one can break in to steal your belongings while you're in a stupor. You make your exit via a personalised pass-code." He shone the torch on a keypad.

"I'm getting cold." It was all she needed to say. He knew just how uneasy she was feeling now, how she wanted to move on. It wasn't somewhere you brought someone you loved after nightfall. He observed her surprise as he closed the lid. He knew, just for a moment, she had feared the worst. Perhaps it was the relief that made her ask a polite question. "So how will this be making you money?"

"I've been pushing the local council for years to think about this and they finally decided to go ahead. They've given me an upfront sum to tidy up the land and start looking at this seriously."

And that was when he saw in her features that she had heard it – the slightest, muffled knocking.

Arthur pointed the remote control at another cylinder and the lid eased open. Through that opening fell a hand. Helen shrieked and might have wanted to run, but her legs were shaking. Perhaps she had also remembered the gate was locked.

Now, with a swift movement, Arthur pulled his shotgun out of the long grass. With the butt he hammered on the hand protruding from the slow-opening cylinder and with a cry the owner withdrew it. Helen had caught sight of him and her hands went to her mouth.

Arthur swung the gun barrel backwards and forwards between them as he spoke. "Helen, meet Paul; Paul, meet

Helen – but I suspect you've already met."

"Oh God! Oh my God! How long has he been in there?"

"Just a few hours. He didn't see me following him on the day of your last liaison. I found where he lived. There's nothing like a gun being wielded by the enraged husband of your lover to convince a man to drive you somewhere in his car."

"Helen, he's mad."

Arthur turned the gun on Paul. "If you shut up, you might still get out of this alive. I just thought you might both appreciate the opportunity to get to know each other a bit better." Now Arthur's features hardened and he gestured at Helen with the barrel of the gun, directing her towards the cylinder in which Paul lay. "In you go."

"What? I..." Helen started to back away. "...no!"

Arthur raised the gun as he had just a few days before. "Just like I told him, there's a chance you might get out of this alive. Disobey me and you won't."

"I can't...I..."

"Nothing stopped you doing what you wanted before." His tone was mocking. "But let me just outline your other option. Nobody knows I own this gun. You die from a shotgun wound and your jealous lover gets a life sentence for the crime. You had mentioned to him that I owned this piece of land, so he then took the keys and tried to hide your body here. I came home, not knowing where you were, happened to see that the keys were missing and mentioned that to the police.

"The choice is yours."

He watched the two of them exchange desperate looks. Were they questioning whether he would go through with it? How he hoped they didn't put him to the test by refusing. Was it an acknowledgement of the time-honoured stupidity of their actions? The one thing he knew those glances did not represent was love. Above all, there must have been regret; an admission that nothing, and no-one, was worth this.

Standing in this eternal triangle was becoming tedious and despite the solitude of that place, there was still the danger that they might be discovered. So he pushed things along: "Five...four...three..." He cocked the hammer of the gun.

Helen raised her hands, shook, shuddered, as did her voice. "Please...Arthur..." How he both pitied and still loved her.

"Two..."

She extricated her heels from the mud and moved towards the cylinder, stopped, turned towards him. "Please!"

At that moment he could as easily have turned the gun on himself – with greater pleasure – and wondered where he found the strength to say: "One!"

In she clambered. There wasn't really room for them to lie next to each other, so she ended up lying on top of Paul.

He needed them to be out of sight now – for his own sake – and pressed the remote.

As the lid started to descend, he said: "Let's see if love is truly eternal."

His words were met with a joint scream of "NO!" One of Helen's arms reached through the opening, likewise one of her lover's as they tried to keep the lid open. It was clear they had decided now it would be better to take their chances with the shotgun than this dreadful torture.

They had left it too long. There wasn't enough space for them to scramble out. The lid continued to close.

Just before the internal light disappeared, Helen let loose a blood-chilling, gut-wrenching cry that tore his heart in two. It was cut short as the lid closed, leaving a void that suggested the universe had pulled the plug of life. The faint knocking that followed was almost a perverse relief. It took all Arthur's willpower not to flick the remote and release them.

At last, somehow, he found the strength to walk back to the car. In he climbed – and his wait began.

So, what would constitute a fitting punishment? Not that it would have been any consolation to his prisoners, but every second that passed tapped at his skull like a water torture. From time to time he flicked on the headlights, unable to deal with the darkness and the way the mass of cylinders brooded in the shadows. He reflected on the fact that, even if his lies turned to reality and the council begged him to develop this site and his product, he could not and would not sanction it.

As the evening edged beyond unbearable, he vowed to return to this place at some future point, destroy his invention and sell the land. The money would be put to better use as the board game appeared to be gaining some momentum.

Now he smacked the heel of his palm against the steering wheel. What the hell was he doing, conjecturing about the future? He had no future…if not with her. Had he not now killed his life with her? She would run at the first opportunity, away from her mad husband.

He looked at the clock: an hour gone. One small hour. It was enough. It would do.

But then the devil leant across from the passenger seat and seared the image of Helen's eyes, closed in ecstasy, onto his memory. *That will never be you, making her so wet,* whispered the unwanted guest – and he was right.

He would give it another hour.

He closed his eyes, knowing that he would never sleep, maybe ever again, and was therefore astonished to wake, to find that exhaustion had taken more of a toll than he had realised.

He pushed open the door to release the voices of revenge from the car and headed towards the cylinders.

*

Their dead bodies were a shock, to put it mildly; hers slumped forward halfway out of the cylinder as the door rose. "What! No! NO!"

He pulled her out, laid her on the grass and searched for a pulse, but it was obvious she was gone. Fumbling for his torch, he looked aghast at the unlit interior of the cylinder. What the hell had happened to the power?

The lingering staleness from that premature tomb assailed his nostrils now. Looking up at the interior, he could see there had been no air. Then the beam of his torch caught the marks on the soundproof lining; scratches where she must have fought to escape. He squeezed his eyes shut.

When he reopened them, he became aware of the preternatural darkness, but it wasn't just a reflection of his soul. He looked towards the distant hulks of the tenements, which in another time might have been a vantage point from which anyone with field-glasses could have seen that night's events, but which had been cleared in recent months in preparation for demolition. The problem was, the city centre beyond them looked the same, comprising nothing at that moment except vague, accusatory shapes. There were no lights. In horror, he realised there had been a power cut. The site here ran off the national grid – in the original plan, the less gruesome version, he had not wanted the possibility of malfunctioning batteries that needed regular charging. Oh, the grim irony of it!

Arthur sank to his knees. "Oh my God! Oh my God!" He rested his forehead on Helen's stomach. "Forgive me – oh please, forgive me! I'm so sorry." Even in his dismay, he heard the irony of those words, mocking echoes of hers as she had lain helpless in the sight-line of his gun barrels in Number Three Merryking Close.

What had he done? What had he done?!

Once again, he lost track of how long he was there. However, at last, he realised he had to come up with a plan.

In the end, it was remarkable in its simplicity.

First, he lifted Helen into the boot of the car, begging silent forgiveness all the while for the need to handle her in that demeaning way. In case anyone had seen them leave together that evening, and given the nosiness of some of his neighbours that was very possible, they would have to return home.

As for her lover...

...Oh for God's sake, give him his name – he was Paul...

...the guy had turned out to be a divorcee with no kids. Here was as good a hiding place as any for the time being.

Not without a considerable strain on his conscience, he closed the lid again and then looked around in the desperate hope nobody was watching. The coast seemed clear.

With headlights off, he drove back out of the gate and then returned to the plot, doing his best to ensure there were no tyre tracks by lifting the grass again with his boots.

As he drove home, all the reasons he might be caught floated around him like wraiths. The presence of his dead wife didn't help. It had to be his imagination, but he could have sworn he felt her weight moving in the back and the paranoia was such, he didn't dare look in the rear-view mirror.

To counteract this, he tried listing the circumstances working in his favour. Helen appeared to have timed her lover's visits to the Close to coincide with the absence of any nosy neighbours. If Paul had talked with any of his friends about his lover, her identity was still doubtless a mystery and if by some freak chance his body was discovered, the fact of it being in the cylinder was not sufficient reason to link his death with Arthur. It would be death by misadventure.

Ah, but Arthur, what if, on discovering his body, the police can work out the time of his death and find it similar to that of your wife? It would be strange, would it not, if someone died of asphyxiation inside your invention at a time and date that coincided with her passing?

He had to push it all aside for now. It could moulder away and doubtless the stench would make itself known later, but he couldn't afford to think about it right now.

As far as Helen's death was concerned...

...he shuddered at the cold objectivity he had brought with such speed into this scenario...

...there had been no violence, nor was there any history of it. This was death by asphyxiation, but not through assault. They would think she died in the night from some sleep apnea-related condition.

One thing over which there would be no need for pretence was his grief. Though he hadn't killed her, he had killed her. He had loved her too and she was dead. Her ghost and his conscience would ensure there would be an echo in the house of every movement she had ever made.

*

That night, everything went sickeningly to plan. He waited until the witching hour and retrieved her from the car. All the other houses were in darkness and he had no reason to believe they were being watched, though he hooked her arm around his waist and acted as if she might have been drunk as he dragged her to and through the door.

Having undressed her and bathed her – details of which Limbo refused to spare him – he had laid her in her bed. If he had thought the hours sitting in his car on the piece of wasteland had dragged, it was as nothing to the night that he then endured. At six o'clock, he could wait no longer and called 999.

Like some plot contrived by the Cecil family, the royal spymasters, to protect Queen Elizabeth the First at any cost, so his plan worked to perfection. Heart failure related to previously undiagnosed sleep apnea was indeed the verdict. There was tension when the disappearance of Paul Machin hit the local headlines, but when he was found in a river some miles away, the verdict of suicide, perhaps a result of the failure of his marriage, was reached pretty quickly. There were no marks on the body to suggest the death had been a violent one.

Arthur was consoled by many, including work colleagues and medical staff, but – and therein started another story – not his neighbours, who either didn't know or pretended not to.

CHAPTER 14

Fifteen years later

Arthur threw back his head and screamed, before feeling what, in Limbo, passed for a chill as he saw that his pain elicited not a single glance from those around him. He knew now, this solitary torment had been foreshadowed in the immediate aftermath of Helen's death, when he might as well have been a lost spirit for all the attention those in the Close had paid to him. While part of him had felt some gratitude that life appeared to carry on along its way, with no fingers of suspicion being pointed at him by public, police, or press, another part must have been hoping for some human interaction to drown out the voice of his conscience. As far as the neighbours would have been aware he had been widowed, so he found himself questioning the innate selfishness of the human condition. If nothing else, surely Helen's absence should have chimed with someone.

Only with the gift of hindsight could he see that the self-pity became his shield; his shelter from the imagined arrows of accusation. Now he saw, when it was too late and he had swapped one lonely vigil for another.

But life and fate had other tricks to play in the form of the success of Chancery. The irony did not escape him – his world became shaped by that dark game, in which everything was driven by truth or lies. Wadsworth Games offered him a huge contract, the money came rolling in – but then, in time, so did the criticisms. As the political correctness of the age took hold, so the idea of people sitting around a board, holding the life or death of someone – albeit small plastic figures – alongside a pair of dice in the palm of their hand, found disfavour amongst the empty vessels who made most noise while the irony of their own judgemental behaviour escaped them. Also, the populace – or so the news would have it – became uncomfortable with the idea of being branded liars for all to see. Thus Wadsworth Games ceased production.

It felt like the rug had been pulled from under Arthur's feet, that his creation was dismantled at the very peak of its fame. He found little solace in the fact that the game took on a cult status. With millions in the bank but his name blackened in the circles which had mattered, Arthur had little to do with his days, especially as he had resigned from his engineering day job, other than to stare through his windows at his uncaring fellow residents. He could have found other employment in all likelihood, but somehow the wallowing seemed to suit his mindset.

His resentment grew and it needed an outlet.

*

And so the years had passed, with Arthur and Number Three Merryking Close starting to resemble each other in their slow decay and isolation, their view of the outside world clouded by dust and cobwebs or resentment and despair. No human visitor broke the solitude. It seemed both property and owner started to be viewed with distaste and suspicion by the other residents. Even the gas and electric meter readers seemed to pick up on the strange aura of the house and just pop a card through without bothering to ring the doorbell. No-one was going to be badgering the owner about having a smart meter installed anytime soon!

The only interaction with another person was that of his conscience with Helen. As the years went on, he believed if he allowed her memory to die, then truly he had no-one. Thus began the strange ritual of keeping her room as it had been on the last day he saw her, complete with the clothes he had laid out for that fateful evening. An observer might have viewed this as a punishment, self-flagellation, this refusal to let the memories die, and Arthur would have concurred – the last two images of her on that bed were of her writhing naked under another man and being lifted lifeless by the undertakers – but the punishment was justified, and in any case, those fragments of his ruin would never fade, just lie in the gathering dust and sand, waiting to be dug up again.

Then, one Christmas, a beacon of light shone through his letterbox in the form of a greetings card from a new neighbour, Andrew Hansen. Daring to dream, Arthur forced himself to step blinking into the light – metaphorical daylight at least, as it was gone five o'clock on a December evening when the young man was returning from work – and plucked up the courage to interact. Andrew seemed pleasant enough, amenable, and Arthur told him he was welcome to pop over for a drink anytime, which Andrew assured him he would.

What had Stoehlheim said days before...? *No wait, it was but hours ago; would Limbo drag its heels zombie-like at this pace forever?* It's not the despair, it's the hope that kills you.

The visit never came. It was the ultimate paradox – through all the darkness of those years, that single act of goodwill by one young man had lit the way to vengeance. Arthur's imagination woke from a long slumber, and the idea came to him. He had observed his neighbours. In fact, he had almost lived a vicarious life through them – though he hated to admit it – and believed he knew the fault lines in their worlds; knew that, for all of them, greed would be an Achilles heel, given the aspirational dreams of anyone who chose to live in the Close. Even Helen herself had been of that ilk, once upon a time.

Arthur had long since come to believe that his Chancery money was filthy lucre; payment by the gods of vengeance for the acts he had committed against his wife and her lover. It was mockery by some demon: *"Here, take this fortune, for spending it will give you no pleasure, nor will you have friends or family to whom you can leave it."* Well, that was about to change. He would find an appropriate recipient.

The project gave him a new lease of life; he had a sense of purpose creating that bespoke board. He felt inspired, as if he were the devil's own engineer. It was a work of genius;

once it was loaded and the hammer cocked – an image worthy of his own dark history – the only things needed were the targets, the amphitheatre of nightmares and the means by which he could draw them all in.

At which point the chill of realisation had passed through him, when it had dawned on him that he would not live to see the game played; to witness his revenge. In so many ways it hadn't mattered while he was engrossed in the process of invention and construction. Now he started looking for tiny faults in the workmanship; flaws that needed mending, refining. Things that delayed the moment of truth. In a moment of abstraction, he felt like he was on a boat travelling an ancient river through thick jungle – the journey would end, but for the time being he would just focus on anything, however small, that needed repair to keep the boat afloat and forget the brooding darkness on either side.

In the end, the thing that helped him to fight through was the awareness that he had felt suicidal often enough. Really there was no-one and nothing to live for – and perhaps he would meet Helen on the other side. Plus, the bottom line was he needed to right many wrongs, both for what he had done to her and to prove and expose the greed and amorality of those around him. There were several parts in this morality play. Their reactions to his death would justify their fates, though the exact nature of those would not be his to know. He knew his own end was deserved. He had, in effect, taken two lives. He might have argued that he had done his time – no second of his life since had contained any joy.

"Come, Arthur," he had said to himself one day, "it's time to get this show on the road. To end this purgatory."

If only he had known.

Heaven or Hell – almost certainly the latter – it mattered not, as it had to be better than this.

If only he had known.

*

Once the masterpiece of his Chancery board was complete, he started the search for an arbiter, an executor...

How the universe was word-playing with him.

...of his will. Given the ethics of solicitors, he'd had no problem picking five names from the directory and spinning a bottle. He ensured the payment he was prepared to make was enough to convince any of those soulless establishments to get the job done properly – not that their standard fees didn't bring them close to that sum anyway. Yet in the light of subsequent events, there was huge irony regarding the price paid. Indeed, in the whole sorry tale, the word *aleatoric* needed literally redefining in the case of Arthur's loaded dice, and *metaphorical* where the ultimate choice of lawyer was concerned. *Random* could now so easily be translated as *meant to be.*

Yet even if he hadn't been the cheapest lawyer, there had been something about Stoehlheim. As simply as that, Arthur knew he would be the perfect overseer of his vengeance. The ruination of these people's lives would be safe in his hands – as it turned out, their afterlives too!

Perhaps he should have read something into Stoehlheim's suggestion that they meet after hours at the lawyer's office. At the time, it suited Arthur's purposes to hide his activities from the world. On reflection, he had been reciprocating that benefit to Stoehlheim. His staff had gone home, and no-one would ever need to know the truth behind the will, or the manner of its execution.

However, more than any of this, it was the lawyer's persuasiveness which had won the day. Before meeting Stoehlheim, Arthur, for all his lack of any faith, had started to believe he might be a lost soul, or one for whom eternal damnation waited, or indeed that he was the devil incarnate. Stoehlheim had reassured him:

"We are the sum of our sins and our mistakes, Mr Du Fuss. There is no goodness in mankind, just the occasional pause in the evil that we do. I find what you are planning here commendable – there is a thunderstorm coming and you are inviting these fools to take shelter beneath the most convenient tree. If they are stupid enough to do so, then they reap the bolt of lightning that follows. Even Mr Hansen, of whom you speak with a certain affection as the only possible winner of the game, will deserve whatever fate throws his way. Perhaps he will simply provide further proof that money cannot buy you happiness. The irony is, as you already know, he gave you hope and took it away – as I said, just a pause in his sinful journey – so perhaps he is even less deserving than the others. I would silence your conscience, Mr Du Fuss; it is simply you giving voice to the possible accusations of the envious and will have no relevance once the first dice are cast."

*

Arthur looked around him now at the stage he had known but would never know again; at people to whom he wanted to scream about the devil and his lies. He thought once more of those whom he had consigned to eternal darkness and wondered, once again for just a moment, whether he was himself the Devil.

"Alea jacta est." He whispered those words, even though he knew none could hear him, nor would they for a time that was indefinable, possibly infinite.

Then he stood and walked away. There was a world, if not his to feel, then at least to observe; a distraction from eternity.

*

Seep Stoehlheim came out into the subdued glow of the main office. There was always a perceptible flicker in the air when he did so, like a static charge, caused by the simultaneous movement of the bowing heads of people suddenly intent upon their work. This never failed to make him smile.

He wandered across to Declan Donaghue's desk. "Mr Donaghue, please ensure that this is delivered by hand."

Declan glanced at the addressee on the envelope – Andrew Hansen.

There was a pause while Stoehlheim stood by the young man's desk. "What is this?"

Declan looked towards where his boss's long finger was pointing and felt himself flush. "It's a doodle, Mr Stoehlheim."

"A doodle?"

"Well, an anagram actually."

"Really?" The sarcasm was unmistakable. "And what inspired this?"

"I...I do a lot of crosswords, Mr Stoehlheim, and those letters sort of leapt off the page at me."

"Unusual."

Something in the lawyer's voice led Declan to believe that he could continue. "You see, I did English literature at school and one of the writers we studied was Christopher Marlowe. So, when the chairman of Wadsworth Games referred in the newspaper here to the tragic passing of the inventor of Chancery, Art Du Fuss, my crossword eyes sort of kicked in with Dr Faustus. I know it's not strictly correct, but..."

"Intriguing," said Sepp Stoehlheim. "Then there will be no need for me to tell you what my name spells." He smiled, then turned back to his office, saying: "It has been a joke in my family for a very long time."

CHAPTER LAST

She could hear whispering – it might have been the breeze passing through treetops and around gravestones, but there were so many sibilant sounds here, including voices, whether those of the living or the dead. They offered words of comfort to the bereaved and accusations towards those not really seen as having suffered a true loss.

She knew she was not part of the group. They could not have made it more apparent, even here at the graveside, where they should have been remembering their beloved son, brother, friend, not leaning in and passing judgement like Claudius' poison into the ears of others. In this place, this reminder of the one immutable fact of human life – death – they stood a little apart from her, even as the coffin was being lowered.

Now the vicar's voice added to the sense of dread, though it was meant, in its way, to offer comfort – a difficult emotion to cling to when you stood amongst ancient trees, which would outlive you, surrounded by damp soil and lichen-covered stone.

"Earth to earth, ashes to ashes, dust to dust: in sure and

certain hope of the resurrection to eternal life through our Lord Jesus Christ."

*

She knew what they were thinking, all of them. It was the main reason she had decided to follow old traditions and wear a veil, from behind which she had been able to observe them all; see the disingenuousness in their eyes as they had offered their commiserations as well as feel it in their limp handshakes. Even during the service, she had ended up pretty much sitting alone and now here, in the graveyard, they were making their slow, awkward retreats. During the burial she had struggled with the knowledge that, in all probability, more than one of them would have liked to push her forward into that hole. She had stepped aside as soon as possible; left them to their grieving and their small-town thoughts.

They glanced at her as they left; daggers of condemnation. *Let them go*, she thought. She had been an outsider all the way and that was never going to change, though a part of her was looking forward to her own dagger twisting during the reading of the will.

She stood alone, perhaps the very embodiment of Thomas Gray's *Elegy Written in a Country Churchyard* – the world had indeed been left to darkness and to her. They were hypocrites, the lot of them.

Look who's talking.

She knew their real issue; the fact that he had made it clear his money was his to do with as he chose. To corrupt Gray's elegy, all of it was being left to darkness and to her.

She had her consolations and her plans.

As if on cue, the wind picked up, whistling now through bare branches and whipping dead leaves into a scuttling motion across the graveyard. She glanced around, half-expecting to see lost souls drifting past the church steeple.

It wasn't fair; she had loved him, if nothing else then during that one night when they had held each other for comfort and ended up making love. It was afterwards that money, as it always did, brought decay and corruption. But wasn't it often misrepresented as a supposed fact that women found power and wealth a turn-on; an aphrodisiac – one as valid as perfume – which was not the natural scent of any female, but was as true a note in the song of love as anything else.

The next whisper she heard was definitive, the voice of her conscience. She looked down into the grave, at the box with its spattering of earth across the top and tried her best to imagine the ashes of her guilt being buried down there too. That wasn't going to be an easy win, even though the fires that heated the forge in which so many lawyers were shaped and sharpened typically sent their morals up in flames.

Still, she had twelve million reasons to feel better – well, a few less now; they had enjoyed life. She just needed to be away from this dampness and all the symbolism of death, with its pretence of an afterlife; escape this whispering.

What her ears had not detected was his approach; the footfall of the man who now seemed to be standing very close behind her – though his words were measured and calm, they caused her to jump. More than any voice, real or imagined, which had reached her ears that morning, this one gave her chills.

"It must have been difficult." Yvonne's response was an attempted segue into quiet sobs, but his next words put paid to that, both by their content and by him allowing the full power of his voice to come through. "Spare yourself the trouble. I meant it must have been difficult having to wait."

Her head jerked round now almost of its own will. "Mr Stoehlheim!"

"At your service, Miss Elmer." He paused and gave a faux courteous nod. "My apologies, I meant Mrs Hansen – or will you be returning to your maiden name for professional reasons?" Again he waited for effect. "Though, of course, you have no need to resume working."

Yvonne lifted her veil to reveal herself. "There's no point in hiding from you."

"Indeed." He gave a knowing smile. "Impossible, in fact."

She looked around, checking that everyone had left, and said: "And no, it wasn't difficult." She gave him a knowing look. "I'm a lawyer; I can play a long game. Besides, he was a good lover." She paused. "And a wealthy one. It made the wait pleasant enough."

Stoehlheim gazed into the clacking December trees. "Still, five years. Given the age gap, you must have been worried that, at some point, his family would have his ear, or your physical charms would desert you before he made an honest

woman of you, inappropriate though that term might be."
When she didn't respond he continued. "You must have
panicked every time some doe-eyed young thing crossed
his path."

She gave a dismissive laugh. "Oh, you know me – I just
invited them to join in. That usually scared them off."

That seemed to amuse Stoehlheim, who chuckled. "Ah,
Miss Elmer – I hope you don't mind if I call you that –
the young are so easy to manipulate, are they not?" He
paused. She knew the question was rhetorical and needed
no response, so gave none. He continued: "But so is all of
mankind... and you are the ultimate proof of that."

It was a puzzling, disturbing comment and Yvonne felt
a defiant streak rising. "What..." Remembering where they
were she looked around and lowered her voice. "...what do
you mean?"

"Miss Elmer, I played you from the moment I saw in you
a kindred spirit."

She felt a chill, despite her latent anger. "Which was when?"

"When you withdrew from the game of Chancery."

"I withdrew because Emma Thomas had approached
me for legal advice regarding her marriage and I was
worried I might be forced to give away some detail..."

He raised a hand and, unusually for her, she stopped.

"Do not take me for a fool, Miss Elmer – that would be
most unwise."

Looking into his eyes now, she saw the absolute truth of
those last words. She had never underestimated Stoehlheim,

but this was the first time there had been such an over-powering sense of latent threat. Why was he here? Did he know her darkest secret? She sensed he did, in which case he held all the cards.

As he continued, Stoehlheim looked around, appearing to take in everything, from the open grave to the ancient tombstones, the winter trees and, beyond them, the grey heavens. The only place his eyes lingered with any hint of questioning was the church steeple.

"I see everything that lurks in the heart of mankind. In you, I saw an instinct for self-preservation." He raised a hand in acknowledgement. "Don't misunderstand me – I was impressed. You recognised destruction when you saw it. With a lawyer's practised eye you saw the game's capacity to destroy. Yet, like some latter-day Shiva, you saw the creativity of destruction and what it might mean for you." Now he looked directly at her again. "And that, Miss Elmer, is when you walked right into my hands..." There was another pregnant pause. "...and those of Arthur Du Fuss."

"That old fool?"

Stoehlheim turned and wandered off a little. As he walked he wagged a finger in admonition. "Therein lay – correction, still lies – his genius. He was too clever for all of you."

Even though Yvonne wasn't having this, she couldn't deny she was feeling an increasing chill for which the December wind was only in part responsible.

"Explain." Her abruptness, the reversion to a lawyer's tone, took Yvonne herself by surprise, but it seemed barely to have registered with this devilish advocate. As Stoehlheim turned around, paced back and came to stand up close in front her, it left her feeling vulnerable and uncomfortable.

"You see, despite a certain fondness for the young man, Mr Du Fuss wanted an element of revenge on Mr Hansen as well and you provided him with the means. Andrew Hansen made the mistake of extending the hand of friend-ship and then withdrawing it from Arthur."

This was the most shocking yet in this series of revela-tions. "You're not serious!"

"Mr Hansen introduced Mr Du Fuss to the agony of hope. He had to be punished and you were the means. I am not saying Mr Du Fuss planned it exactly as it happened – that has been my pleasure to arrange. The others were arbiters of their own fates." Now Stoehlheim put his fingers to his chin in thoughtful manner. "The crone and Miss O'Reilly were meant for each other, though clearly the latter thought the same about you." Here he winked at Yvonne and like all his supposed gestures of conspiratorial matiness, it had the opposite effect as Yvonne felt a layer of ice settle on her bones. "Mr Thomas was always going to kill his wife and her lover – whoever that proved to be. He was disturbed enough that his suicide was also inevitable. But once Mr Hansen proved not to be Mrs Thomas' lover that left a dilemma for Arthur – what punishment would fit his crime? And there you were, much to my satisfaction. A young man who acquires money beyond his dreams and a woman capable of ruining him, one way or the other. A perfect storm."

Yvonne frowned. "So what was all that bullshit in the preamble before the game about the winner not being subject to Arthur's curse?"

"Oh, if you knew what became of the others..." Stoehlheim laughed, a disturbing sound as he looked down into the grave. "At least Mr Hansen can rest in peace. In a strange way, I think Mr Du Fuss would have approved of that."

"You make it all sound preordained." Yvonne gave a snort of slight derision.

Stoehlheim looked up again and into her eyes once more. She saw only darkness. "And so it was, once you all sat around that table. Of course the cards were stacked." He was dismissive and waved his hand to emphasise that. "Those dice... beautiful pieces of work. They contained the tiniest of hollows in which little bearings moved, weighted to fall with apparent randomness, which was in fact engineered precision. The devil himself would have been proud of them. And Mr Du Fuss had been an engineer before he found fortune and despair. It is why the rules for that final game specified that everyone would throw in the order of their house numbers."

"But the double sixes..."

"Planned. Think of the cards that awaited each of those players."

Despite having witnessed extremes of duplicity in her career, Yvonne was struggling to fathom such cunning. "He couldn't have witnessed every episode on which the questions were based."

"No – but I could."

As chilling responses went, it took some beating. Yvonne started to feel herself going under, disorientated. Then she saw a line and grasped for it. "You – neither of you – could have foreseen that I would stand down from the game. Your order of dice-throwing would have been ruined by that."

Yvonne felt sudden vindication and with it, some strength returned. Never mind *Home Truths* and *Little White Lies* – she had just grasped those cards and dealt a winning hand.

To her intense disappointment, Stoehlheim didn't even hesitate. "I'm afraid we did, Miss Elmer, or at least I did. I knew professional etiquette would prevent you – if you remember that evening and that moment, I hazarded a guess at your reasons before you volunteered them. If you had decided to let your conscience go to hell, I would have raised the topic myself; found a way to make your participation untenable in the eyes of the other players."

That floored her – but she was not a lawyer for no reason. Yvonne might have been down, but she wasn't out and threw a final blow. "Andrew...my husband never really remembered how he responded to that final *Home Truths* card, so how could he have been guaranteed to answer truthfully?"

Stoehlheim smiled in a way befitting someone who knew the game was over and he stood victorious. "Mr Hansen's Bible would have turned green even if he had announced that he was the Devil himself." He paused. "All of you paid the price for failing to see the smouldering fire that burned in Number Three Merryking Close."

"I don't believe you." It was pure bravado on her part and he saw through that.

"Your eyes and shaking voice tell me otherwise." He leant in close to her face. "Is it so hard to twist someone to your will and whims? You did it."

Yvonne tried to look puzzled and uncomprehending, but she was no longer even fooling herself.

"How many times, when Mr Hansen suggested he should make a will leaving money to family and charities, did you manage to divert him, leaving you sole heir?" He looked deep into Yvonne's eyes, deeper than anyone had in her entire life. She held his gaze, but at last she wavered. She looked towards the coffin and he followed her gaze. "Was it at least difficult to see him die?"

*

She cannot be sure whether in some surreal way Stoehlheim has led her to this. After all, though it goes against everything she believes in, or rather her lack of any belief or faith, she feels there is more to him than the dust from which the rest of humanity is made. It is as if she is standing outside herself, observing the events of that evening.

She can hear the waves pounding way down below at the base of the cliffs as the Atlantic vents its eternal spleen, even on this beautiful night with its calming sunset.

She and Andrew are weaving a little drunken path, arm in arm, along the top of the cliffs. He is carrying a bottle of the single malt that has become his drink of choice. She removes herself from his embrace as he heads closer to the cliff edge. The lines are a little blurred. Was this a plan, or at this point just self-preservation?

He turns and slurs: "C'mon, don't be a wimp."

"No way!" She laughs, but stays where she is. Andrew stops and stands facing the sea. He nearly overbalances for no good reason, regains his footing and then launches into uproarious laughter, before growing a little thoughtful.

"Night falling; no-one for miles around except the woman I love." He turns, gives her a drunken wave, and then stares out again. "A good supply of alcohol. The mighty anger of the sea, which has no conscience... perfect, eh?"

She agrees. "Perfect." She is suddenly behind him. She pushes him. Andrew plunges over the edge into the huge drop.

There's no time to lose. She calls the police, knowing she will be believed – she has no motive and is a professional in the law. As long as they get him to the mortuary they will find a level of alcohol in his blood that backs her story.

It's a tragic accident.

*

Yvonne turned back to Stoehlheim. "No, when all's said and done, it wasn't difficult." She felt like he had been watching her the entire time.

Now he shook his head.

"If it was that easy to take a soul, then we are indeed alike, as I suspected." He stepped away for a moment. Looking to the heavens, he closed his eyes and seemed lost in thought. On opening them again, he addressed the horizon, though his words were intended for her. "I have been asked over the years, who is the other Stoehlheim?" He turned to her again. "It is every man. In every generation, I have found someone to aid me." He paused. "Someone to play devil's advocate, if you like. Who better than a lawyer?" He came and stood in front of her again. "Thank you."

"For what?" She was taken aback. A 'thank you' from Stoehlheim was like a gift from a creepy uncle.

"For proving, once again, that there will always be a place in this universe for me."

He stepped forward and despite herself, Yvonne took a wary step back. He continued: "And now, I think it is time to discuss my payment."

Yvonne gave a slight smile and felt like she was back on firm ground. "I guess I had a feeling you would be here today." She opened her handbag, fumbled around inside and withdrew an envelope. Holding it towards Stoehlheim, both of them could see how her hand shook. "It's funny, you know, I always thought I would argue about this, as I understand you already had a huge payout, but now I just want you to take it and leave me alone. It's twenty per cent. I hope you think that's fair."

"Very." Stoehlheim took the envelope, examining it with an almost exaggerated thoughtfulness before tossing it like a thing of no consequence into the open grave with much theatrical disdain. He didn't even bother to watch its descent.

Yvonne looked on aghast. "What are you doing?!"

"As you rightly pointed out, I took my commission some time ago." Yvonne put down her handbag. She stood at the edge of the grave, tottering in the loose earth as she considered how best to lower herself in and retrieve the cheque. She made to remove her heels. "So quick to join him?" Stoehlheim smiled. "Perfect..." He paused. "...to use your final word on the cliff top."

Now Yvonne paused and looked up, shocked. "How did you...?" It was horrifying to feel as if the thoughts and memories of moments before had somehow been read.

At last, she saw the truth, and there was horror in the realisation and the moment.

He gestured with an incline of the head towards the grave. "Retrieve your money, if you must." Now he moved to stand in front of her once more. He leaned in and a warmth other than his breath brushed her skin. "I have another payment in mind and it can wait for as long as it must...for so can I. As you said, we lawyers can play a long game, but I have outplayed them all."

Held by his gaze, she saw something that terrified her. It caused her to back away. He took another step towards her and pointed to Andrew's coffin. "Believe me, you will wish you could join him. Mankind has always failed to understand the true significance of 'R.I.P.'."

Yvonne turned, just about remembering to pick up her handbag, but leaving the cheque, and started to hurry from the cemetery. She reached the gate and was about to open it...

"Miss Elmer!"

...but she stopped at the sound of his voice, turned with great reluctance. "Do not keep me waiting."

Her eyes widened, full of fear and confusion. Turning again, head down, she hurried through the gate and started to cross the road to her car.

There was a screeching of tyres.

Yvonne looked up, horrified, just as a van smashed into her. She flew backwards with the impact and landed on her back. Blood trickled from her mouth as she lay with her eyes closed.

*

Stoehlheim knew the unfortunate driver of the van would have to live with what he had done for the rest of his life, even though it was not his fault – but the key thing was he would live.

*

That driver leapt from his van and crouched in distress by the side of Yvonne, before reaching into his pocket for his phone. He looked up and around him while he waited for the emergency call to be answered, though even to his untrained eye it was obvious that it was already too late. Looking towards the church, he wondered exactly what had caused her to rush out in that way. He saw nothing and no-one.

*

Yvonne Elmer's time in the eternity of Hell begins as it will continue, in blackness and silence. Her eyes fly open; the pupils are dilated. Her face is white, while all around her is the colour of obsidian. It begs the question, if black is the only colour in your world, does it cease to be a colour? She sits up, looks around, blind panic distorting her features. She opens her mouth, screams, but no sound comes out; it is a soundless black hole. Again, she screams – again, there is only silence. Hell, it seems, defies and challenges our definitions, for can something soundless be a scream? She struggles to her feet, her body bent and misshapen, while her hands feel for and touch those injuries, to her horror. Of course, she cannot know this is how she will spend eternity. She starts to stagger forward, whatever forward means, hands moving from her wounds and reaching for something, anything definable in the darkness. Always there is that infernal oxymoron, the silent scream, as she goes on her way.

*

Sepp Stoehlheim observed all of this, standing with one hand resting on his computer screen, bent forward, looking intently at the images it displayed, those of Yvonne's lurching, silent progress through that utter void.

At one point, as her face filled the screen, staring, screaming, Stoehlheim looked away from it towards the picture of Munch's *The Scream* that hung on his office wall. He gave a slight nod in its direction. Then he straightened up, made a gesture with his hand across the screen and it shut down. Straightening his jacket, he turned and left the room.

THE END